新编商务英语

口语教程 **1**

（第二版）

Business English
Interactive Speaking
(Second Edition)

XINBIAN SHANGWU YINGYU KOUYU JIAOCHENG

总主编　虞苏美　　张春柏

主　编　杨乾龙

编　者　李　晨　　丁卓君
　　　　杨　明　　田　崖

高等教育出版社·北京

HIGHER EDUCATION PRESS　BEIJING

图书在版编目（CIP）数据

新编商务英语（第二版）口语教程.1 ／ 虞苏美，张春柏主编；杨乾龙分册主编. －－2 版. －－北京 ：高等教育出版社,2011.11

ISBN 978－7－04－032978－0

Ⅰ . ①新… Ⅱ . ①虞… ②张… ③杨… Ⅲ . ①商务－英语－口语－高等职业教育－教材 Ⅳ . ①H319.9

中国版本图书馆 CIP 数据核字（2011）第 211114 号

| 策划编辑 | 陈锡镖 | 责任编辑 | 贺 刚 | 封面设计 | 顾凌芝 | 责任印制 | 韩 刚 |

出版发行	高等教育出版社	网　　址	http://www.hep.edu.cn
社　　址	北京市西城区德外大街 4 号		http://www.hep.com.cn
邮政编码	100120	网上订购	http://www.landraco.com
印　　刷	北京汇林印务有限公司		http://www.landraco.com.cn
开　　本	850mm×1168mm　1/16		
印　　张	12.75	版　　次	2004 年 8 月第 1 版
			2011 年 11 月第 2 版
字　　数	333 千字	印　　次	2011 年 11 月第 1 次印刷
购书热线	010-58581118	定　　价	32.00 元（含光盘）
咨询电话	400-810-0598		

前　言

　　近年来,越来越多的外语教育专家和教师认识到外语学习的目标应该有两个:即把某一种外语作为"知识"来学习,或把这一种外语作为"交际工具"来学习。前者主要以"语法"为重点研究对象和以"精确"为评估标准,引导学生将绝大部分精力和时间用于对句子结构的分析和比较。因此,以"知识"为学习目标的外语专业学生有能力把目标语的各种句子结构和语言特色评析得头头是道,但不一定有能力将他的评析用目标语完整清晰地表达出来。社会上流传的所谓"哑巴英语"的说法也是这种学习目标的定位结果。对我国的绝大部分外语专业的学生来说,外语学习的目标无疑应是"交际工具"。对于这部分学生,教师只有把外语学习的重点落实在提高学生的目标语运用能力上,才有可能将学生真正置于一种近似的"自然语言学习环境"中,通过"学会表达"——"正确表达"——"清晰正确表达"——"完整清晰正确表达"这样一种循序渐进的自然过程,达到全面提高学生交际能力的教学目标。

　　《新编商务英语(第二版)口语教程》以心理学、教育学和外语学习理论为编写的指导思想,在语言材料选用和课文结构设计上贯穿了"学用结合,重在运用"的原则。课文内容着重反映当代日常和现实商务活动的真实情景,练习活动丰富,实用性强。本教材虽然是专门为学习商务英语的高等院校的学生而设计和编写的,但也可用作非商务英语专业学生的教材和英语爱好者的自学课本。

　　本教材全部课文围绕一个美国商人 Henry White 一家在中国和英美等国的日常生活和商务活动展开,涉及经济、贸易、工农业、教育、旅游、投资、金融、劳务、地产等领域中的考察、谈判、签约、网上交易、电子商务等等。每个单元都有一个中心话题和与话题相关的课堂练习活动,旨在促使学生将口语学习不仅仅停留在传统的机械背诵和模仿上,而是通过大量的任务型课堂活动来强化英语语言的运用能力,使英语真正成为表达学生个人情感和思想的"交际工具"。

　　为了更好地与高中英语教学大纲衔接,本教材第一册主要为各种日常会话,对话的地点主要安排在国内,背景则是中国学生所熟悉的各种口语交际活动的场所。内容主要涉及介绍相识、电话交流、谈论天气、邀请聚会、用餐、购物、看病、吉庆假日、娱乐、邮寄包裹和体育运动等日常生活领域中的用语。从第二册起,大部分对话的地点和背景将移向国外,商务活动内容逐渐增多。这种结构上的安排为学生对背景和专业知识的了解,提供了一个从"熟悉"到"不熟悉"的渐进过程,从而使英语学习能以难点分散、反复巩固、循序渐进的螺旋上升方式进行。

　　《新编商务英语(第二版)口语教程》共分 4 册,总教学课时为 360 学时,每册为 90 学时。第一、第二册各为 16 单元,第三、第四册各为 15 单元。

　　本教材第一册每一单元分为四大部分:热身练习(Warm-Up)、样板对话(Dialogues)、交际功能范句(Functional Expressions)和交际任务(Communicative Task)。其中热身练习、样板对话和交际功能范句的内容都有配套的录音。

第一部分是热身练习,主要供学生在正式上课前以个人或小组为单位进行练习之用,目的是使学生迅速地过渡到英语语言环境。

第二部分是样板对话,供教师和学生在课堂上使用。对话语言生动活泼,口语特点鲜明,人物活动的情节引人入胜。对话示范性地展示了各种日常和商务活动场合中的英语口语表达的结构和方式,使学生能在较短的时间内掌握准确且得体的日常和商务口语。

第三部分是交际功能范句,这部分旨在向学生提供某一语言交际功能中可以使用的各种表达方式。需要指出的是:虽然在某一功能下,有各种各样的句子可供说话者选用,但是,这并不等于说,说话者为了完成某一功能而可以随意"挑"一个句子说说就行。在很多情况下,会话的场合、会话双方的社会地位和身份以及讲话的目的决定了只有某一个句子才是这种特定会话环境中最恰当的表达语;而在某些情况下,用不同的语气和语调说出同一个句子,则表达了说话者完全不同的意思。这种句意与语气、语调之间的微妙关系,需要在教师的指导下,经过较长时间的学习才能掌握。

第四部分为交际任务,这些任务均与对话主题或交际功能相关。这是本教材区别于许多其他英语口语教材的重要特点之一。这种交际任务为学生提供了一个检验自己学习成果和在现实生活中实践英语语言运用能力的机会。样板对话和交际功能范句的学习是进行交际活动的基础,交际任务又是学生对样板对话和交际功能范句消化吸收和对英语语言规则内化的一个必不可少的语言习得步骤。在进行交际活动时,教师应特别注意学生中可能出现的重语言形式、轻言语意义和在课堂上机械地模仿样板对话和交际功能范句的"伪交际"现象。在以语法翻译法和听说法为主要教学方法的中学英语课堂上,这种现象是屡见不鲜的。为了减少和避免"伪交际"现象,教师应尽量为课堂交际任务的活动提供真实的实践背景和必要的语言词汇,在教学中提高学生语言技能运用的时间比例,使学生逐步学会和掌握表达自己想要表达的真实思想和观点。必要时,教师可以因地制宜地对本部分交际任务的活动内容作适当的修正。

总之,我们希望学生通过对本教材的学习,不仅能听懂日常和商务英语会话,能以准确的语调进行英语会话,自由地表达自己的思想和观点;而且能逐步养成用符合特定场合的得体语言回答或者提出各种问题的习惯,为今后的工作做好充分准备。

在编写本教材过程中,我们得到了国内外同行的启示和高等教育出版社编辑的帮助。英籍专家 Frank Tonge 协助审阅了本教材的全部语言文字并参与了部分课文的编写工作。在此,对所有关心、支持和帮助本书编写和出版的人员,表示衷心的感谢。

由于编者水平和经验有限,本书可能有疏漏和不当之处,我们诚恳希望外语教育专家和使用本书的广大师生不吝指教。为此,我们特开设与外语教育专家和使用本教材的广大师生交流的网上平台:http://v2.my99.us/sms/,欢迎大家积极参与。

编 者

2011 年 8 月于华东师范大学

Contents ▪▪▪▪▫

Unit One

Introducing

 Warm Up

1. Say out Loud and Fast

1) I think I should begin by introducing myself.

2) I should take the liberty of introducing her to my admirable aunt.

3) I introduced my country cousin to the city by showing him the sight.

4) Tobacco was introduced into Europe in the sixteenth century.

5) The government introduced universal secondary education a decade ago.

6) She introduced permanent social and medical reforms in English life.

7) Shakespeare always introduced some comic relief into his tragedies.

8) One after another, she was introduced to newly arrived business partners.

9) He introduced me to the fascinating world of the retail IT business.

10) The company is introducing a new family saloon this year.

2. Culture Tip

When people are being introduced in very formal situations, you may have noticed that rank is the most important consideration followed by age then sex. Therefore, people of a lower rank should be introduced to people of a higher rank first; younger people should be introduced to older people first; and men should be introduced to women first.

Most conversations, however, are not carried on in formal speech situations, and forms of address are another important decision to make. A social acquaintance or a newly hired colleague of approximately the same age and rank is usually introduced on a first name basis.

You should also add some information about the people being introduced to help start the conversation.

It is polite and common to shake hands when people are introduced to each other in China. But in the United States or some other countries, people don't always do so. However, in a formal or business situation, people almost always shake hands whatever their nationality.

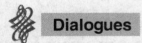 **Dialogues**

Dialogue A   Small World

Mr. Henry White is walking down a street in Shanghai. Suddenly he sees his old friend Dan Jackson in front of him. He and Dan haven't met each other since they left college.

Henry: Dan! Hello, Dan. It's me, Henry.

Dan: Yes, oh, yes. Hi, Henry. So good to see you again after so many years. It's a small world, ha!

Henry: Fancy meeting you here, Dan! Where have you been all these years?

Dan: I've been working in the Citibank since I left college. How's everything with you?

Henry: Well, I got married soon after I left college. I worked in a consulting company New York for about five years before I came to China. Now I'm the General Manager of Shanghai Computer Company.

Dan: Great! Congratulations! Are you here by yourself?

Henry: No. My wife and my son are with me. You must come and visit us sometime.

Dan: I'd love to. But not today, I'm afraid.

Henry: Sure, whenever you're free. Here is my phone number and address. Give me a call before you come.

Dan: Oh yeah, I will. Well, I guess I must get going. Bye then.

Henry: Bye.

(*Three days later. Dan Jackson is now visiting Mr. White and his family.*)

Henry: Sophia, I'd like you to meet my friend Dan Jackson. Dan and I went to college together. Dan, this is my wife, Sophia.

Sophia: How do you do, Mr. Jackson? It's a great pleasure to meet you. Henry often talks about you.

Dan: How do you do, Mrs. White?

Sophia: Call me Sophia, please.

Dan: I'm very glad to meet you, Sophia.

Henry: And this is my son, Richard.

Richard: Hello, nice to meet you.

Dan: Hello. Richard.

Henry: I have a daughter, Isabel. She's now at school in America. Here's her picture.

Dan: She looks like you and she's beautiful. I think you have a nice family.

Henry: It's nice of you to say so.

Sophia: Would you like some coffee, Mr. Jackson?

Dan: Oh, yes. But Dan, please.

Henry: OK. Let's sit down and have some coffee.

Dialogue B   A Favor

There is a knock at the door. Sophia goes to open the door and sees a young man standing there with a colorful box in his left hand.

Hugh: Good afternoon. You must be Mrs. White.

Sophia: Yes. And you are ...

Hugh: My name is Hugh Fox. I'm here to visit Richard. Is he in?

Sophia: Yes, he is. Come in, please. Richard, your friend is here.

Richard: Hi, Hugh.

Hugh: Hi, Richard.

Richard: I don't think you've met my dad, Hugh. This is my dad. And Dad, this is Hugh, my friend.

Hugh: How do you do, Mr. White? I'm glad to meet you.

Henry: Hello. I'm glad to meet you, too.

Richard: And I think you've met my mom, haven't you?

Hugh: No. Nice to meet you, Mrs. White.

Sophia: Pleased to meet you, Hugh. Please sit down and make yourself at home. Would you like to have any drink? Coffee or tea?

Hugh: Tea, no sugar, please.

Richard: I get it for you. We got organic tea from Hangzhou.

Hugh: Thank you very much. Richard, do you still work in the Shanghai Advertising Company?

Richard: Yes. Pretty soon our company will open five subsidiaries and extend the business to a global scale and advertising will become one of them. What are you up to?

Hugh: I wonder if you can do me a favor.

Richard: Sure. What can I do for you?

Hugh: You see, our factory is going to introduce a new toy into the market. And my boss asked me to find an advertising agent to help us promote the toy.

Richard: Well, you've found the right person.

Hugh: Good. Here is the new product. Have a look at it.

(*Hugh opens the box and takes out a funny toy.*)

Richard: What a nice toy! I think it will sell well.

Hugh: Of course, this kind of toy sells quite well in many places in Europe.

Richard: And your boss's thinking of exploring into the Shanghai market?

Hugh: Yes, but our factory is a newly built one, almost unknown to the consumers here.

Richard: I see. But I don't think it's going to be a problem. There is a potential market for toys in Shanghai as well as in other parts of China. The one-child policy encourages almost every family to treat their child like a king.

Hugh: I know. That's why we're pretty confident about our products.

Richard: You mean you will continue to sell other toys?

Hugh: Definitely. And we want to make sure our first product is a big success here.

Richard: I see what you mean. Come on, let's go to my room and work out the details for this funny but wisely designed toy.

Hugh: OK. Will you excuse us, Mr. and Mrs. White?

Sophia: Go ahead and good luck to your new venture.

Hugh: I need it. Thank you, Mrs. White.

Dialogue C Visit to a Toy Company

Today Hugh Fox and Richard White are in the office of Hugh's boss. They are going to talk about the details for advertising the newly produced toy.

Hugh: Ms. Wu, this is my friend Mr. Richard White from the Shanghai Advertising Company. Richard, this is Ms. Fudi Wu, our General Manager.

Ms. Wu: How do you do, Mr. White? I'm so glad you can come.

Richard: How do you do, Ms. Wu? Nice to meet you.

Hugh: Ms. Wu, Richard is my good friend. He's agreed to help us with our advertising.

Ms. Wu: That's good. Have you talked to him about the toys?

Hugh: Yes. We have talked about the advertising. Richard has some nice ideas about it. Would you introduce your plan, Richard?

Richard: All right. Ms. Wu, the toys are very attractive. My idea is that we get some boys and girls to play with these toys in some public places, like the People's Square, the Bund, shopping centers and amusement parks. Their laughter and cheers will certainly draw the crowds. What do you think?

Ms. Wu: Great!

Hugh: I think we need some kind of background music for it and a band to play the music. Are you able to arrange that?

Richard: OK. I'll ask someone to compose a bright jingle and background music for it. In fact, we have a musician working for us at the moment. I'll talk to him about it.

Ms. Wu: Can you tell me roughly how much the cost would be?

Richard: How much are you prepared to spend?

Ms. Wu: As long as it helps us sell our products, we're ready to pay for it.

Richard: Good. I'll talk to my business partners and we'll draft a proposal. Then we can meet again to discuss more details including the cost.

Ms. Wu: When do you think you'll be ready with the proposal?

Richard: It'll take about a week, I think. That's next Tuesday.

Ms. Wu: Great! So we'll meet again then. Thank you very much for your time, Mr. White.

Richard: It's a pleasure.

Ms. Wu: Give me a call when the proposal is ready. We can have lunch together next Tuesday if you like.

Richard: OK. See you next Tuesday.

Hugh: (*Follows Richard out of the office.*) Thank you, Richard.

Richard: You're welcome.

Hugh: Would you care for a drink?

Richard: I'm afraid I have to go. I'm introducing my girlfriend to my parents this evening.

Hugh: Awesome. I'm sure they will like her.

Richard: I'll keep you updated. Bye.

Hugh: Bye.

Dialogue D   Richard's Girlfriend

Richard has a girlfriend, who is a ballerina. It's Tuesday evening. Richard brings his girlfriend, Ying Xu, home to meet his parents:

Richard: Mom, Dad, this is Ying Xu.

Ying: How do you do, Mr. and Mrs. White?

Henry: How do you do?

Sophia: Nice to meet you, Miss Xu. Richard told us that you are in the Shanghai Ballet. How long have you been learning ballet?

Ying: Almost 11 years. I joined the Shanghai Ballet three years ago.

Henry: It must be hard to be a ballet dancer, isn't it?

Ying: Sometimes it is. You see, I often have no holidays for weeks and have to travel a lot. We're always giving performances in different cities and different countries. But I love ballet. After these years everything else is not a big problem for me anymore.

Richard: Ying is busy all year round but we still can find time to be together.

Sophia: Well, that's nice.

Ying: Yes, we try to make time in our schedules.

Henry: Well, we're glad you could make it tonight.

Ying: Richard and I bought some small watermelons on the way home. It's a new variety for the season. Have you tried it?

Sophia: Oh, yes. It is very sweet and juicy.

Richard: I'll go and get a knife.

Ying: I'll help you to wash them.

(Richard and Ying leave the sitting room.)

Henry: Ying is a very nice girl. I like her. I think Richard has found a good daughter-in-law for us.

Sophia: Well, It's too early to say so.

Henry: What do you mean?

Sophia: Many of my friends tell me girls in Shanghai are pretty picky.

Henry: Are they? I don't think so. Many American girls are choosy, too.

(Two hours later.)

Ying: It's been very late. I have to leave now. Thank you so much for inviting me.

Sophia: Thanks for coming. You know, you're always welcome. Do come and see us when you're free.

Ying: I will, if it's not inconvenient. Goodbye.

Henry & Sophia: Goodbye.

Notes

1. Citibank	(美国)花旗银行
2. consulting company	咨询公司
3. whenever you're free	什么时候有空都行
4. yeah	是的
5. call at	拜访

6. call me Sophia	叫我索菲娅好了
7. advertising agent	广告代理商
8. organic tea	有机茶
9. subsidiary	分公司
10. What are you up to?	怎么了? 有什么事吗?
11. promote	促销
12. You've found the right person.	你可找对人了。
13. sell well	畅销
14. exploring into the Shanghai market	进入上海市场
15. consumer	消费者;用户
16. potential market	潜在的市场
17. treat one's child like a king	像对待国王一样地对待孩子
18. be confident about	对……有信心
19. definitely	当然
20. Will you excuse us?	请原谅,我们要离开一会。
21. venture	风险投资
22. public place	公共场所
23. shopping center	(区域)商业中心
24. amusement park	游乐场
25. jingle	广告歌曲
26. draft a proposal	起草协议文本
27. if you like	你愿意的话
28. Would you care for a drink?	喝一杯,怎么样?
29. awesome	棒极了
30. ballerina	芭蕾舞女演员
31. the Shanghai Ballet	上海芭蕾舞团
32. It must be hard to be a ballet dancer.	当芭蕾舞演员想必是很辛苦的。
33. get together	相聚
34. make time in our schedules	挤出时间来
35. picky	好挑剔的;过分讲究的
36. choosy	好挑剔的;慎重选择的

 Functional Expressions

Introducing Somebody

1. By the way, do you know each other? John Brown, Susan Smith.

2. Do you know Mr. Carl Monad? Mr. Monad is the Chairman of Alfa Club.

3. Have you met Nathan Malcolm, Cathy?

4. Hey, here's David. David, meet John.

5. I don't think you've met each other before. This is my sister, Anna. Anna, this is my friend Frank Jackson.

6. I'd like to introduce to you our director, Mr. Dongling Gao.

7. Ladies and gentlemen, allow me to introduce to you Mrs. Jenny Samson, Chairman of the World Wild Life Fund.

8. Let me introduce to you Mr. John Grant, President of the China-Britain Business Association.

9. Look, here's John! John Tom. John, this is Jane, Jane Brown.

10. May I introduce Mr. Stanley Young, Assistant Manager of General Electric?

11. Meet my brother, Walker.

12. Mr. Lynx, I want you to meet Mr. Naomi Service, the director of Cambridge Research Institute.

13. Oh look, Wendy's here. Wendy, come and meet Whitman.

14. Richard, I'd like you to meet Sheila Rhoda, a famous film star in Hollywood.

Introducing Yourself

1. Allow me to introduce myself. Jenny Heywood, an engineer from General Motors.

2. Excuse me. I don't believe we've met. I'm Edgar Snow.

3. Excuse me, my name's Sidney Carson.

4. Hello! Isaac Livingstone. I'm Tony Johnson.

5. How do you do? I'm John West.

6. How do you do? My name's Steven White.

Responding to an Introduction

1. Glad to see you.

2. Happy to meet you.

3. How do you do? I'm Teresa Spencer.

4. It's a pleasure to meet you.

5. I've known so much about you.

6. I've often heard about you.

7. I've wanted to meet you.

8. Pleased to know you.

Asking Somebody's Name

1. Are you Mr. Eden?

2. Aren't you Mrs. Clarke?

3. Could you let me know your name?

4. I believe you're Mr. Jackson, aren't you?

5. May I have your name, please?

6. May I know your name?

7. What are you going to call the baby?

8. What's your name, please?

9. You must be Mr. Edmond.

Communicative Task

Welcome to Our College Party

Types of Task: pairs, whole class.

Functions Practiced: introducing yourself and someone else, responding to others.

Pre-task

1. Look at the following table only at this moment. Do not look at other tables at the end of this Unit.

2. Work with your pair to figure out the genders of the following Common First Names and complete this table, using F for female and M for male.

Common First Names

First Name	Gender	First Name	Gender	First Name	Gender
Adam		Agatha		Alan	
Amanda		Amelia		Amy	
Arnold		Blanch		Carol	
Catherine		Cecilia		Charles	
Daphne		Dennis		Diana	
Douglas		Emily		Ernest	
Felix		Frank		Freda	
Gilbert		Gordon		Grace	
Helen		Henry		Herbert	
Hilary		Howard		Ida	
Isabel		Jane		Jason	

continued

First Name	Gender	First Name	Gender	First Name	Gender
John		Joseph		Judy	
Justin		Kelly		Kendrick	
Lilybell		Linda		Louis	
Luke		Mark		Mary	
Melvin		Michael		Monica	
Nancy		Nicholas		Oliver	
Oscar		Paul		Pearl	
Philip		Rebecca		Richard	
Rose		Rosemary		Rudolph	
Samuel		Sandra		Sebastian	
Sophia		Stephen		Stewart	
Sylvia		Teresa		Thomas	
Vanessa		Victor		Victoria	
Viola		Walter		Wendy	

3. Check your completed table with your pair and confirm that both of you have the right answers. At this step，you are allowed to use your dictionary if necessary.

4. Work with your pair to read the table below to get yourself familiar with the meanings of these common first names.

Meanings of Selected Common English First Names

First Name	Meaning	First Name	Meaning
Adam	human, mortal	Kendrick	royal ruler
Agatha	the good	Leo	the lion
Amy	beloved	Lilybell	fair lily
Amelia	industrious	Linda	beautiful
Amanda	worthy of love	Louis	famous in battle
Alan	comely, fair	Lucy	light
Alice	noble	Luke	light
Carter	cart-driver	Mark	God of war
Blanch	white，fair	Mary	bitter in Hebrew
Charles	man，greatness	Maurice	dark-skinned

continued

First Name	Meaning	First Name	Meaning
Dennis	Greek god of wine	Melvin	chief
Douglas	dweller by the dark stream	Michael	look like lord
Carol	song of joy	Monica	adviser
Arnold	mighty as the eagle	Morgan	born by the sea
Catherine	pure	Nancy	grace
Andrew	manly	Nicholas	people's victory
Ernest	intent in purpose	Oliver	peaceful
Cecilia	sky	Olivia	the olive (peace)
George	farmer, husbandman	Oscar	leaping warrior
Frank	free	Paul	little
Cynthia	title of moon goddess	Pearl	the pearl, gem
Felix	fortunate	Peter	rock
Gilbert	illustrious pledge	Philip	lover of horses
Daphne	the laurel tree	Rebecca	snare, firm binding
Gordon	hero, brave man	Richard	powerful ruler
Grant	great	Robin	of shining fame
Diana	goddess of the moon	Rose	a rose
Doris	a sea goddess	Rosemary	dew of the sea
Henry	ruler of the home	Rudolph	far-famed wolf
Emily	industrious	Ruth	a friend, beauty
Herbert	bright warrior	Samuel	asked of god
Eve	life	Sandra	helper of mankind
Howard	chief warden or guardian	Sebastian	the revered
Isaac	the laugher	Simon	heard
Grace	the graceful	Sophia	wisdom
Jason	the healer	Stephen	a crown or garland
John	God's gracious gift	Stewart	keeper of estate
Helen	light, pretty girl	Susan	a lily
Freda	peaceful	Sylvia	forest maiden
Hester	a star	Teresa	the harvester

continued

11

First Name	Meaning	First Name	Meaning
Joseph	Lord shall add	Thomas	the twin
Hilary	pleasant	Toni	beyond praise
Ida	happy	Vanessa	butterfly
Julia	youthful	Victor	the conqueror
Isabel	consecrated to god	Victoria	the victorious
Justin	the just，upright	Vincent	conquering
Jane	God's gracious gift	Viola	violet
Kelly	female soldier	Walter	mighty warrior
Jennifer	white wave	Wendy	brave girl
Judy	the praised	Winifred	friend of peace

Task Procedure

1. Select one name that you like most for yourself as your new identity for your English class.

2. Make an ID（Identification）card for yourself with a piece of paper（10 cm long and 6 cm wide）.

3. On your new ID card write your selected English name with meaning and pronunciation（if possible）on the top lines，followed by your personal information such as age，hometown，previous school，dormitory room number，hobby，phone number and/or e-mail，etc.

4. Now welcome to the College Party begins. With the name card on your shirt or jacket，move around to meet your fellow students by using the sentence patterns and functional expressions you have learned in this unit or in your high school.

5. Introduce yourself to others and/or introduce your fellow students you have just known to others.

6. Invite your teacher to join you in the party. You may ask your teacher if he/she has an English name. If your teacher does not have an English name，select a name for your teacher from the list and explain to your teacher and the whole class why you have selected this name.

7. You can also ask your fellow students questions about the particular names they have chosen for themselves，such as "What does your name mean?" or "Why did you choose this name?"

8. After the party is over，teacher may ask some students to introduce themselves to

class and some of their fellow students they just came to know.

A Complete List of Common First Names

Female First Names

First Name	Meaning	First Name	Meaning
Agatha	the good	Julia	youthful
Amanda	worthy of love	Kelly	female soldier
Amy	beloved	Lilybell	fair lily
Amelia	industrious	Linda	beautiful
Alice	noble	Lucy	light
Blanch	white, fair	Mary	bitter in Hebrew
Carol	song of joy	Monica	adviser
Catherine	pure	Nancy	grace
Cecilia	sky	Olivia	the olive (peace)
Cynthia	title of moon goddess	Pearl	the pearl, gem
Daphne	the laurel tree	Rebecca	snare, firm binding
Diana	goddess of the moon	Rose	a rose
Doris	a sea goddess	Rosemary	dew of the sea
Emily	industrious	Ruth	a friend, beauty
Eve	life	Sandra	helper of mankind
Grace	graceful	Sophia	wisdom
Helen	light, pretty girl	Susan	a lily
Freda	peaceful	Sylvia	forest maiden
Hester	a star	Teresa	the harvester
Hilary	pleasant	Toni	beyond praise
Ida	happy	Vanessa	butterfly
Isabel	consecrated to God	Victoria	the victorious
Jane	God's gracious gift	Viola	violet
Jennifer	white wave	Wendy	brave girl
Judy	the praised	Winifred	friend of peace

Male First Names

First Name	Meaning	First Name	Meaning
Adam	human, mortal	Luke	light
Alan	comely, fair	Louis	famous in battle
Andrew	manly	Nicholas	people's victory
Arnold	mighty as the eagle	Morgan	born by the sea
Carter	cart-driver	Mark	God of war
Charles	man, greatness	Maurice	dark-skinned
Dennis	Greek god of wine	Melvin	chief
Douglas	dweller by the dark stream	Michael	look like Lord
Ernest	intent in purpose	Oliver	peaceful
Felix	fortunate	Peter	rock
Frank	free	Paul	little
George	farmer, husbandman	Oscar	leaping warrior
Gilbert	illustrious pledge	Philip	lover of horses
Gordon	hero, brave man	Richard	powerful ruler
Grant	great	Robin	of shining fame
Henry	ruler of the home	Rudolph	far-famed wolf
Herbert	bright warrior	Samuel	asked of God
Howard	chief warden or guardian	Sebastian	the revered
Isaac	the laugher	Simon	heard
Jason	the healer	Stephen	a crown or garland
John	God's gracious gift	Stewart	keeper of estate
Joseph	Lord shall add	Thomas	the twin
Justin	the just, upright	Victor	the conqueror
Kendrick	royal ruler	Vincent	conquering
Leo	the lion	Walter	mighty warrior

Unit Two

Greeting

 Warm Up

1. Say out Loud and Fast

1) The old man managed to wheeze out a greeting, and then began to cry.
2) Every new announcement of hers was greeted with shouts of laughter.
3) The Hebrews greeted us with a friendly wave of the hands.
4) Her new novel was greeted by reviewers with rapturous applause.
5) If I should meet you after long years, how should I greet you?
6) They'll hold a get-together to exchange greetings at the weekend.
7) There'll be a meet-and -greet event for newly recruited employers.
8) Those girls greet one another with a warm kiss.
9) The greeting cards are finely made with rich colors and humorous patterns.
10) These Chinese conventional greetings, however, need careful studies.

2. Culture Tip

Generally speaking, there are two kinds of greetings: special greetings and everyday greetings. The former refers to the greetings used on special occasions, such as "Happy New Year!" and "Merry Christmas!". The latter refers to the greetings used every day, for example "Good morning." and "How are you?"

Forms of address are also important in English speech community. You are obliged to address certain people by their social identity in formal situations: public officials (Congressman or Your Honor), educators (Professor or Doctor), leaders of meetings (Mr. Chairman), Roman Catholic priests (Father Gansberg), nuns (Sister Anna), and so forth.

You may have also noticed that native speakers tend to say "Nice to meet you" more often than "How do you do" although they don't know each other before.

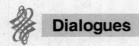

Dialogues

Dialogue A   A Neighbor

On his way home Henry meets his colleague, Dongbao Wang, who lives in the same neighborhood as Henry. Mr. Wang caught a bad cold two weeks ago and has been on sick leave for six days.

Henry: Good evening, Mr. Wang. How are you going?

Mr. Wang: Good evening, Mr. White. I'm much better now. I've been taking Chinese herbs, twice a day. It looks like Coke but tastes bitter. Most importantly, it works for me.

Henry: I'm glad to hear that. Do you need to visit your doctor again?

Mr. Wang: Yes, I have an appointment with the doctor next Tuesday morning. If he says OK, I can go back to work then. By the way, how's the new product testing going?

Henry: The testing is going very well with the schedule. We have tested every detail as we planed. We need to make sure that everything is perfect. We can't afford a single small mistake. It is expected to be the most profitable product we've ever designed.

Mr. Wang: Yes, I understand. I remember a few weeks ago, when I was still in the office, we found a small flaw in the graphic card. We worked very hard for two days to correct it.

Henry: That's true. I do appreciate your hard work during the testing period. Only staff as experienced as you can identify and fix such a critical problem.

Mr. Wang: Thank you, Mr. White. I'm just doing my job.

Henry: I really enjoy working with you. Everyone in the Testing Department misses you.

Mr. Wang: I'm eager to plunge myself into the task of new product testing. I'll go back to work as soon as I recover.

Henry: That's good. But no pressure on anything. It's pretty cold at this time of the year. Take good care of yourself and keep warm at night.

Mr. Wang: Thank you very much, Mr. White. I will take care of myself. As I feel much better now, you can let my colleagues know that they can call me if there is anything urgent coming up with the testing.

Henry: That's good. I'll let them know the minute I step into the office tomorrow morning. We are lucky to have you in the team.

Mr. Wang: It's my pleasure.

Henry: Well, I guess I must be leaving now. My stomach's sending signals.

Mr. Wang: It's nice to talk to you, Mr. White. Have a good night.

Henry: Thank you. You have a good night too.

Dialogue B A Busy Morning

It is the Labor Day today, one of the Federal Holidays in the United States. This is also a great occasion for a family reunion as well as the time to invite best friends to get together.

Sophia: Happy Labor Day!

Henry: The same to you. Are you doing anything special?

Sophia: I'm having some friends come over. We're going to have dinner with them at home.

Henry: Shall I help you to get everything ready for the party?

Sophia: Sure. Go upstairs and get a tablecloth and a set of wine glasses.

Henry: OK.

(*A few minutes later.*)

Henry: Sophia, here are the glasses and the tablecloth you want. What else can I do for you?

Sophia: Em. Let me see. We've got some beef, vegetables and wine. But I couldn't find a single turkey in the market this morning. Would you please go to the Metro Supermarket to get one?

Henry: A turkey? Yes, of course, a turkey for the Labor Day dinner. It wouldn't be a Labor Day dinner without a turkey, as your mother says. Shall I buy a big one or a small one?

Sophia: A large one please, because there'll be eight people tonight.

Henry: As you wish. What else do you need for the dinner?

Sophia: Well, a box of lollies and some fruit. That'll be good enough to make a perfect Labor Day dinner.

Sophia: By the way, on your way back home, will you go to Helen's house and invite her and her husband to come to our house this afternoon?

Henry: Why not ring her?

Sophia: I tried to ring her several times this morning, but nobody answered. There must have been something wrong with her telephone. She is at home, I'm sure.

Henry: OK, I'll go there and invite them to come over. Anything else?

Sophia: That's all, darling. Are you going by bike or on foot?

Henry: By bike. It'll take me at least twenty-five minutes to walk. That's too much for me. Besides, Helen's house is on the other end of the street.

Sophia: But be careful while you're riding in the streets. The other day I saw a woman was badly injured in a terrible bike accident not far from the Metro Supermarket.

Henry: Don't scare me, please, sweetheart. I'm not a good rider, but I've kept a good safety record for about two years. You know that, don't you? I'll be back shortly.

Sophia: No rush, take your time.

Dialogue C   A Greeting at Home

The doorbell rings. Sophia goes to open the door. Two of her colleagues come to pay a visit. One is Nancy Carson, and the other is Helen King.

Sophia: Good afternoon.

Nancy: Good afternoon, Sophia.

Helen: Good afternoon. Nice to see you, Sophia.

Sophia: Come in and have a seat and make yourself at home. Nancy, how is your husband?

Nancy: He's very well. He has made a quick recovery from pneumothorax and will be back to work in a few weeks. Tonight he'll fly to Shanghai with Helen's husband.

Sophia: That's great. Ask them to come over and join us tonight, please.

Nancy: Thank you for the invitation.

Helen: They'll be happy to have Labor Day dinner with all of us.

Sophia: That'll be our honor. Helen, did you have a good time when you visited the Summer Palace in Beijing last week?

Helen: Yes. Beijing is one of the most beautiful cities in the world. I enjoyed it very much. I think we might go there together sometime next year.

Nancy: That's a good idea. I wish I could go there this year.

Helen: It's not good for us to go to Beijing in winter. It's a bit too cold there. How are your parents in Washington, Sophia?

Sophia: They're quite well. My father retired three months ago and does some gardening every day. My mother still does housework at home and sometimes goes out to dance in the nearby club.

Nancy:	She's a good dancer. She once taught me to dance when I visited you in your hometown five years ago.
Helen:	Yes, she's very kind and enthusiastic. Please say hello to your parents for us.
Sophia:	OK. But would you like some coffee and cake? Tonight we'll have tuna salad, roast beef, sweet and sour pork ribs, and the most important main dish, of course, the roast turkey for dinner. What do you think?
Nancy:	It sounds more than great to me!
Helen:	I love roust turkey. It certainly will remind me of the typical Labor Day dinner at home.
Sophia:	Henry is preparing coffee for us in the kitchen. He's good at that.
Helen:	Yes, I can tell from the smell. It makes me even thirstier. Tell him we're already here.
	(*Just at that time, Henry comes out from the kitchen with a tray of cups.*)
Henry:	Ladies, I know, I know. Welcome and happy Labor Day! Coffee's ready. This one is for you, Helen and this is yours, Nancy.
Nancy &	
Helen:	Thank you very much.

Dialogue D   A Labor Day Dinner

It's the evening of Labor Day. Richard and his girlfriend return home early. Sophia has invited four friends to be with her family to observe their first Labor Day in China at home.

Richard:	Mum, Dad, we're home. Where are you?
Henry:	(*Busy with cooking in the kitchen*) I'm in the kitchen.
Ying &	
Richard:	Happy Labor Day!
Henry:	Happy Labor Day to both of you. Come and help me. There'll be eight of us for dinner tonight.
Richard:	Where is Mum?
Henry:	She is chatting with her friends in the sitting room.
Richard:	What can we help you with?
Henry:	Wash these dishes and plates, put the turkey into the oven and pour the boiling water into the teapot.

Ying: Let me pour the water and do the washing. I don't know how to cook turkey in an oven. Chinese people don't eat turkey very often.

Richard: I'll do it. But after we get married, you'll have to get used to many Western customs, I'm afraid.

Ying: I'll be happy to try my best to get used to them. But be patient with me. It takes time, I'm afraid, too.

Richard: Yes, ma'am! Now come with me. It's time for us to say hello to the guests tonight. Helen and her husband, Tom, and Nancy and her husband, James.

Ying: OK. After I finish the dishes and plates.

(*A few minutes later.*)

Richard: Happy Labor Day, everyone! Pleased to see you again.

Ying: Happy Labor Day! Glad to meet you here, Helen and Tom.

Helen: Hi there, Ying. Nice to see you again.

Tom: It's been a long time. How are things going with you?

Ying: Couldn't be better, thanks, Tom.

Nancy: Happy Labor Day! Ying, this is my husband, James.

James: How do you do? It's my honor to meet our princess of the night at this homely occasion.

Ying: My honor too. Nice to meet you. (*Turn to everyone.*) I got tickets for all of you. *The White Hair Girl*, a Chinese classic ballet performed in Grand Theater tomorrow night.

James: Oh, boy! Ballet is the favorite one by all of us, I guess. Thank you, my princess.

Nancy: Ah, yes, thank you, my dear!

Tom: A surprise! We are lucky to have this opportunity to enjoy a Chinese ballet.

Helen: Hey! I didn't expect to watch a ballet. Thank you very much. We all will have a special and wonderful holiday.

(*Twenty minutes later, the dinner begins.*)

Sophia: I'm very glad to have so many friends to celebrate the holiday with our family. You are all welcome here. Happy Labor Day to everybody! Cheers!

All: Cheers!

Henry: Help yourself. Authentic home made food, I guarantee.

Sophia: Henry took cooking courses in high school. He cooked all the dishes for us tonight. Well, it's time for us to judge Henry's cooking skills.

Helen: Mmmm. Delicious, amazing and great. The roast turkey tastes super. It reminds me of the dinner Tom and I had in Denver five years ago.

Tom: Right. Exactly the same taste. And the sweet and sour pork ribs are terrific，too. Henry，you should run a restaurant and it'll make you a millionaire overnight，I believe.

Henry: Thank you. I'll think about it.

Notes

1.	colleague	同事
2.	on sick leave	休病假
3.	Chinese herbs	中草药
4.	profitable	有利润的,赢利的
5.	graphic card	计算机图形卡,显卡
6.	plunge somebody into	全力投身于……
7.	I'm just doing my job.	我只是尽责而已。
8.	no pressure on anything	不要给你自己任何的压力
9.	something urgent that comes up	出现紧急情况
10.	My stomach's sending signals.	我肚子呱呱叫了。
11.	Labor Day	劳动节(美国)
12.	family reunion	全家团聚
13.	on the occasion	在这种场合下
14.	turkey	火鸡
15.	the Metro Supermarket	麦德龙超市
16.	a box of lollies	一盒子什锦糖果
17.	That's all.	就那些了。
18.	ride	骑(自行车)
19.	No rush.	别着急。
20.	take your time	慢慢来
21.	pneumothorax	气胸
22.	gardening	园艺;种花养草
23.	enthusiastic	热心的
24.	It sounds more than great to me!	听上去好得不得了了。
25.	sweet and sour pork ribs	糖醋排骨
26.	oven	烤箱;烤炉
27.	observe	庆祝
28.	Cheers!	干杯!
29.	authentic	真的;真正的
30.	home-made food	家常菜

31. Denver	丹佛市(美国科罗拉多州)
32. millionaire	百万富翁

 ## Functional Expressions

Greeting Somebody

1. Ah，Dave. Just the man I was looking for.
2. Bumping into you like that was a bit of luck.
3. Glad to meet you here，Toni.
4. Haven't run into you for ages.
5. Haven't seen you for some time.
6. Hello, Emily.
7. Hi there, Charles!
8. Hi, Sandra. Just the person I wanted to see.
9. How are you，Steven?
10. How is your new job?
11. Howdy，my dear friends?
12. I'm so glad you could come to my sister's birthday party.
13. It was good to see you again.
14. It's been a long time.
15. Long time no see!
16. Nice having you come to my wedding.
17. Pleased to meet you，Louis.
18. Pleased to see you again.
19. Small world，isn't it?
20. This is a pleasant surprise!
21. What brings you here today?

Stating How You Are

1. All right，thank you.
2. As usual.
3. Can't complain.
4. Could be better，but not bad.
5. Couldn't be better，thanks.
6. Fine，just fine.
7. Fine，thanks.

8. I am just so-so.
9. I am much better.
10. I am very well.
11. I'm fine. Thank you.
12. I'm full of the joys of spring.
13. I'm just great.
14. I'm on top of the world, thanks.
15. I'm very well indeed, thank you.
16. Much better, thank you.
17. No complaints.
18. No, nothing much.
19. Not too bad, thanks.
20. Oh, the usual rounds.
21. Pretty fair, thanks.
22. Pretty good, thank you.
23. Quite well, thank you.
24. Really fine.
25. Same as ever.
26. So-so, thanks.
27. Still alive — just not at all well.
28. Very well, thank you.
29. Well, not too good yet. Better than I was though.

Asking After Somebody
1. Anything new?
2. Are you better?
3. Are you feeling better now?
4. Are you well?
5. How are things going with you?
6. How are things?
7. How are you doing?
8. How are you keeping?
9. How was everything with you?
10. How was your weekend?
11. In good shape, are you?
12. What are you doing these days?
13. What are you up to these days?
14. What's happening to you?

15. What's new with you?
16. What's new?
17. What's the news?

 ## Communicative Task

My Family Tree

Types of Task: pair.

Functions Practiced: greeting, introducing, asking for relations, apologizing.

Pre-task

1. Look up in your dictionary for the definition of "family tree".
2. Write the definition here

_____

_____

3. The following diagram shows what a family tree looks like. Figure out the relationship between "Me" and other members in the diagram.

A Family Tree

Davi — Jane

Peter — Eve   Doris — Ada   Charle — Eileen   Anne

Susan   Clare — Paul   John — Rose   Donn — Steven   Ian

Emm — Robert   Alice   ME   Leo   Sara — Kevin

Pearl   Luke

4. Fill out the table below according to the above diagram.

Table of Family Relationship

Name	Relation to "ME"	Name	Relation to "ME"
Adam		Alice	
Charles		Anne	Grandaunt on my mother's side
David	great-grandfather	Clare	
Ian		Donna	
John		Doris	
Kevin		Eileen	
Leo		Emma	
Luke		Eve	
Paul		Jane	
Peter		Pearl	
Robert		Rose	
Steven		Sarah	
	ME	Susan	

5. Find out your answer to the final question "Who am I?" by filling out the blanks with the correct member of the family in the following 8 statements. Check your answers based on the relations shown in the family tree diagram below.

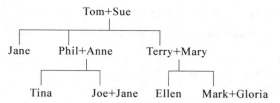

1. My <u>father</u> is 64 years old. His name is <u>Tom</u>.
2. My _____ is 62. Her name is _____ .
3. I have got a _____ , she is 37.
4. My _____ is 40. He is married with two _____ .
5. I have got two _____ , too.
6. My _____ is called _____ . She is 17 years old.
7. My _____ is called Joe. He is married.
8. His _____ is called _____ , just like my _____ .
   Who am I? My name is _____ .

Task Procedure

1. Compare your finished table and your answer to the question "Who am I?" with your pair's to see if both of you agree with each other. Do not forget to use greeting formulas to start your conversation.

2. Take out a clean sheet of paper and write your own name in the middle of the sheet to draw out your own family tree.

3. You have 5 minutes to draw as much your family tree as possible.

4. When the time is up, whether or not you have finished your family tree, you exchange your complete or incomplete family tree diagram with your pair.

5. In turns, you and your pair ask each other questions about both of your families and use the answers to complete your pair's family tree. Jot down extra information if necessary. For example:

Did your great-grandfather have any brothers?

Does the husband of your mother's sister have any nephews?

Was your cousin on your mother's side married?

What are your nephews' names?

6. Based on the completed tree, ask your pair some more questions about his family members. For example:

hobbies　favorite drinks
sports　date of birthday

7. Select one of your pair's family members you would like to visit and ask your pair to do that part. So now, the conversation goes on between you and one of your pair's family members. Remember you begin your conversation with introducing yourself, greeting, small talk and then move to the main topic that you know both you and your pair's family member are interested in.

8. Reverse the roles and do Step 7 again.

Unit Three

Weather

Warm Up

1. Say out Loud and Fast

1) Why the river is not frozen in such a cold weather is still a question.

2) If the Lord gives us clear weather, I think I can do it.

3) A glass of beer in the hot weather sure hits the spot.

4) This mansion is built to stand any weather.

5) The wind and the waves have weathered the rocks on the shore.

6) They reacted to the appalling weather with typical British stoicism.

7) Tight shoes and hot weather are the causes of tenderness of the feet.

8) The movement of water is also an important weathering force.

9) The price of vegetables fluctuates according to the weather.

10) Our weatherboards are truly an Australian classic, providing the warmth, versatility and a smart look of real timber.

2. Culture Tip

A very common way to start a conversation in English-speaking countries is to talk about the weather. There is a ubiquitous saying in those cultures, "Mentioning weather can be an inoffensive way to start a conversation under any circumstances."

Strangers often talk about the weather in order to warm up the atmosphere and break the ice. In this way, people can get to know each other naturally and continue to talk about other subjects.

When you are traveling or working abroad, remember that there is considerable variation in climate all over the world so that you may avoid some embarrassing situations.

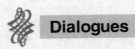 **Dialogues**

Dialogue A   Weather Forecast

Henry is going to take part in an important conference today. When he looks out of the window, it is rather cloudy. Henry talks with his wife about the weather and he believes it is going to rain.

Henry: Honey, did you watch the weathercast on TV last night? How is the weather today?

Sophia: Yes. It should be a fine day today according to the weather report. The chance for raining is only 10%.

Henry: Oh, nonsense! It's going to rain today, I am sure. Look at the sky, full of heavy dark clouds. I am a hundred percent sure we're going to get some thunder storm in the afternoon, if not in the morning.

Sophia: Well, I am not as sure as you are, although sometimes weather forecast may fail due to unpredictable air currents, you know. Where are you going this morning?

Henry: There's an important business conference in Pudong and I'll stay there for about three days. Shall I take an umbrella with me? Just in case.

Sophia: Sure. And put an extra jacket in your suitcase, please. Perhaps after a heavy rain, it'll be much colder there.

Henry: Oh, yeah, you're right. By the way, what do you think of the weather in Shanghai?

Sophia: I like spring, summer and fall. It's warm and fine in spring, summer and fall, and I can go swimming in the outdoor pools almost 9 months around the year, though it's a bit hot and muggy in summer. But fall is terrific. I love fall here. And I now fully understand why people here name it the Golden Fall; it's much more than just a season for harvesting.

Henry: Yeh, I know what you mean.

Sophia: I don't like winter here. It's too wet and miserable.

Henry: I think the weather in Shanghai is always changeable though, especially in spring and fall.

Sophia: But on the whole, it's better than that in our hometown, isn't it?

Henry: You're right.

Sophia: I've been used to the changeable weather in Shanghai already.

Henry: But not me. I think it'll take a little longer for me to get used to it.

Sophia:	I'm leaving for office now. By the way, don't forget to buy some fresh flowers on your way back home. There is a large flower market in Pudong, next to the Red Star Hotel. I need them for my party this weekend.
Henry:	What a coincidence that I'm going to stay in the Red Star Hotel! Roses or lilies?
Sophia:	Either of them will do, I don't mind. Oh, I have to go. Breakfast is ready on the table. Take care of yourself.
Henry:	You too.

Dialogue B   Weather and Water Saving

It is raining very hard now. Sophia returns home and hears Richard showering in the bathroom.

Sophia:	Is that you are taking shower, Richard?
Richard:	Yes. I got wet from top to toe on my way home. What a terrible day it is today!
Sophia:	And tomorrow, too. It's going to be cloudy and windy tomorrow, the weatherman says.
Richard:	(*Comes out of the bathroom.*) Well, I wish that the worst of the season will be over soon.
Sophia:	Put on more clothes. Only 12℃ in the sitting room.
Richard:	All right. Shall I turn on the air conditioner?
Sophia:	You ought to have turned it on before you took the shower.
Richard:	What time does the weathercast begin on TV?
Sophia:	At six o'clock sharp in the morning.
Richard:	I see. That's why I missed it. Too early in the morning. Maybe Dad will get wet too.
Sophia:	He won't come back home until Thursday. He's out on a business trip and has an umbrella with him. He knew the bad weather before his leaving.
Richard:	Mom, Jason sent an e-mail to us last night.
Sophia:	Your uncle? Haven't heard from him for long time. What did he say?
Richard:	He said there was a destructive cyclone and then a severe flooding after in Brisbane. Twenty people died and hundreds lost their homes in the flood.
Sophia:	Really? My God. Twenty died? In Brisbane? Brisbane is the capital of Queensland and the third most populous city in Australia. You know?
Richard:	I know. Jason said that's the death toll in the floods in whole state of Queensland not just in Brisbane itself. And he also mentioned that it was the

worst flood in history since 70s.

Sophia: What about his family and his house?

Richard: They are fine now. Their basement was flooded and water was up to knees, though.

Sophia: That was bad enough. Bad luck for Australia. I feel sorry for Australia people. Last year they got the worst bush fires due to the dry weather and this year they hit with the worst storm and floods. It's abnormal, isn't it?

Richard: Yes, it is abnormal. Do you remember last year just before the bush fire Jason called us and told us he had installed those tap aerators to save water because of the heavy drought lasting continuously for 10 years.

Sophia: Of course, I remember that. He told us there was little water in many rivers and hundreds of creeks were dried out. Some reservoirs had only less than 12% of water.

Richard: Many local governments in Victoria even put a fine on watering the home lawn and garden using tap water. One of my Chinese friends took a business trip to Melbourne two years ago, he saw many labels on local residential garden fences, saying "Recycle water in use" or "Rainfall from roof collected to water my garden". At the first sight he thought local people were doing it to protect their environment until later he got to know the story of water restriction and fines issued by the local government.

Sophia: Jason also mentioned Victoria government had forbidden car washing at home to save reservoirs. Otherwise, they would have got into troubles in water supply. Installing tap aerators is a very good idea to save water in kitchen and bathroom.

Richard: Of course. We should install some in our apartment. A tap aerator or a faucet aerator is often found at the tip of modern indoor water faucets. Without an aerator, water usually flows out of a faucet as one big stream. An aerator spreads this stream into many little droplets. This helps save water and reduce splashing.

Sophia: Ah, you seem to know a lot about it.

Richard: Trust me. I do know a lot about it. To tell you the truth, if we had the tap aerator installed on our showering faucet, I could have saved 3 gallons of water this evening. The amount of water passing through the aerator is measured by Gallons Per Minute (GPM) in the United States; the lower the GPM the more water the aerator will conserve.

Sophia: In Shanghai, people use liters instead of gallons. One gallon is approximately 3.79 liters. That means you wasted about 11 liters tonight or we waste about 30 liters of water every day. Am I right?

Richard: You are absolutely right, my dear Mom.

Sophia: Then the first thing you'll do tomorrow is to get this water saving aerator, my smart son.

Richard: Yes, Madam.

Dialogue C   Harbin in Winter

Henry is having a meeting in Pudong. He is staying in the Red Star Hotel there. He has made many friends from different parts of China. After lunch, he sits in the lobby, talking with Mr. Gao, the head of a computer company in Hangzhou.

Henry: It's been raining for two days already.

Mr. Gao: It's awful, isn't it?

Henry: Yes. You're from Shanghai, aren't you?

Mr. Gao: No, I'm from Hangzhou. I was born in Harbin, but left at 12 when my parents moved to Hangzhou. I've been living in Hangzhou for more than thirty years.

Henry: Are you accustomed to the weather here?

Mr. Gao: Yes. I like the weather in Shanghai. It's neither very hot in summer nor too cold in winter. Anyway, I like living in cities along the coast.

Henry: Don't you think it's wet and a little chilly these days?

Mr. Gao: It rarely rains and snows in winter here. But if you go to Harbin, the climate is quite different.

Henry: Have you ever been to Harbin since you left at 12?

Mr. Gao: Yep. My parents moved back to Harbin ten years ago. I go and visit my parents every year during Spring Festivals. Have you been to Harbin?

Henry: I haven't been to any city in the north. What's the weather like in Harbin in winter?

Mr. Gao: It's very cold, dry and freezing.

Henry: How do people there spend their winter days?

Mr. Gao: More or less the same as in summer. Although it is cold in winter, outdoor activities are just as fun as those in summer. During snowing days people do stay indoors with air conditioners or heating facilities, but activities on ice and snow give them extra fun which people here are longing for.

Henry: I was told that lakes and rivers in Heilongjiang are frozen in winter and people walk on the iced surface of the river from one side to the other.

Mr. Gao: That's true. I had that experience in my childhood. I skated a lot on rivers and lakes with my friends.

Henry: Really? I'm very interested in Harbin and I think I might have to make a plan to visit Harbin some day.

Mr. Gao: It's worth seeing Harbin by yourself.

Henry: Do you think winter is the best time for me to visit there?

Mr. Gao: Of course. It's great fun to visit Harbin in winter. You'll find how relaxed you are when you are skating on a lake, with natural landscape surrounding you and warm sunshine embracing you. Besides, Harbin is famous for ice sculpture and ice lantern show.

Henry: That sounds interesting. I guess my wife will also be interested in visiting Harbin in winter. Well, it's ten to one. We must go back to the conference. It's been nice talking to you, Mr. Gao.

Mr. Gao: My pleasure. See you later.

Henry: Yep, see you later.

Dialogue D   Flood and Drought

Sophia, Helen and Nancy are in their office and talking about flood and drought.

Sophia: Helen, look out of the window. It's literally pouring. I wonder when it's going to stop.

Helen: The weather has been terrible these days in many parts of China, you know.

Nancy: Right. It's been raining for a long time in the South, while a drought for a few months in the northern part of China.

Sophia: Some rivers in the northern China have dried up completely. But have you heard there is a terrible flood in Jiangxi Province?

Helen: No. Tell us about it.

Sophia: Yes, many places in the province are totally submerged. Some villages are engulfed by the flood.

Nancy: Any deaths?

Sophia: Yes, some were drowned.

Nancy: Didn't they know the flood was coming?

Sophia: The government had warned them of the flooding. But for some reasons they decided to stay. Then the tragedy happened.

Helen: How about those people in the flooded areas now?

Sophia: The paper says the soldiers are striving to save those people's lives. I'm sure they'll be safe.

Helen: Sometimes I just wonder why there is no way to prevent natural disasters from destroying people's lives, houses, lands, and so on.

Sophia: Technology is far from being perfect to keep disasters like flood from doing harm to people and their properties. It seems always to just give us what we do not want and refuses to give us what we need. But we just have to live with it.

Nancy: You are right. We just have to live with it. Hey! Look，it's stopped raining.

Helen: According to the weather forecast，it'll be fine tomorrow. Shall we take our tourists to Hangzhou as planned?

Sophia: Since it's going to be fine tomorrow and no one has called to cancel the trip，I think we'll go with the original plan，but we should tell the drivers to be more cautious.

Nancy: I got a fax from Hangzhou. They say there will be a fog over the West Lake for the next three days. Shall we still take them to Hangzhou?

Sophia: Yes，but delete the sailing on the West Lake from the program list. It is important to keep our tourists safe.

Nancy: OK. I'll put a poster on the door straightaway and send a short message to our tourist group.

Notes

1. a ubiquitous saying	普遍存在的说法
2. inoffensive	不冒犯人的；不伤人的
3. break the ice	打破沉默
4. conference	（通常持续几天的）大型会议或研讨会
5. nonsense	胡说八道
6. What do you think of . . .?	你认为……怎么样?
7. hot and muggy	又热又闷的
8. yeh（= yes）	是；而且
9. wet and miserable	令人沮丧的阴雨连绵（天气）
10. on the whole	大体上，基本上
11. what a coincidence that . . .	真是太巧了……
12. Either of them.	哪个都行。
13. wet from top to toe	从头到脚都淋湿了
14. keep an umbrella in the office	在办公室里备把伞
15. At six o'clock sharp.	六点整。
16. on a business trip	出差
17. a severe flooding after	随后就是一场洪水

18. cyclone	(澳洲)海上飓风
19. Brisbane	布里斯班市(澳大利亚)
20. Queensland	昆士兰州(澳大利亚)
21. death toll	死亡人数
22. bush fire	森林火灾
23. abnormal	反常的
24. tap aerator	自来水龙头的节水装置
25. creek	小溪
26. Victoria	维多利亚州(澳大利亚)
27. recycle water	雨水,再生水,循环使用的水
28. water restriction and fines	用水限制与罚款规定
29. faucet	自来水龙头
30. little droplets	小水珠
31. splashing	(水的)飞溅或泼洒
32. conserve	节省
33. lobby	大厅;休息室
34. the head of a computer company	一家计算机公司的领导
35. left at 12	12 岁时就离开了
36. heating facilities	取暖设备
37. natural landscape	自然风光
38. warm sunshine embracing you	温煦的阳光照在你身上
39. ice sculpture and ice lantern show	冰雕冰灯展览会
40. flood and drought	洪水与干旱
41. totally submerged	完全被水淹没了
42. engulfed by the flood	被洪水吞没了
43. strive to save	奋力抢救
44. go with the original plan	按原计划进行
45. delete the sailing on the West Lake	取消在西湖上的游船活动

 ## Functional Expressions

Asking About the Weather

1. Do you know the weather update?
2. How is the weather today?
3. How is the weather, Nicholas?
4. What do you think of the weather, Joe?

5. What does the weather look like?

6. What is the weather forecast for tomorrow?

7. What is the weather like today?

8. What sort of day is it?

Stating How the Weather Is or Will Be

1. It is drizzling/raining/pouring/blowing hard/clearing up/freezing now.

2. It is getting cold.

3. It is supposed to be cloudy this afternoon.

4. It is warm/mild/sunny/fair/splendid/perfect/hot/sultry/muggy/cloudy/foggy/breezy/ windy/cool/chilly/cold/frosty/snowy/wet/damp/dull/gloomy/oppressive/wretched/nasty.

5. It looks as if a storm is coming.

6. It looks like snowing/raining/hailing/sleeting this afternoon.

7. It'll probably turn warm tomorrow.

8. It's a clear/lovely/warm and nice/scorching/boiling/miserable/rotten/wet/beastly/ snowy day.

9. It's an awful day, isn't it?

10. It's very likely to have a downpour in a short time.

11. It'll apparently turn out to be a misty day.

12. It'll seemingly continue to be fine.

13. It'll snow soon, without a doubt.

14. The radio says it's going to be a fine day tomorrow.

15. The weatherman says it's going to rain the day after tomorrow.

16. There is a typhoon/hurricane/tornado coming.

17. There'll be a gale tomorrow.

18. We'll get a shower in a few minutes, I'm sure.

Communicative Task

Weather Information

Types of Task: pair, group.

Functions Practiced: talking about the weather, seeking and sorting information, weather reporting, giving cautions and clarifying.

Pre-task

1. Here are some additional nouns and adjectives that are most commonly used when people talk about weather.

2. Discuss with your pair some words or phrases you are interested in. Make sure both of you can pronounce them correctly and know how to use them.

atmosphere	大气;空气;气氛	awful	糟糕的
beastly	令人讨厌的	blow dust	扬沙
blow hard	刮大风	boiling	沸腾的
breezy	有微风的	chilly	寒冷的
clear up	放晴	climate	气候
cloudy	多云的,阴天的	cyclone	旋风;飓风;暴风(澳大利亚)
damp	潮湿的	dew	露水
downpour	倾盆大雨	drizzle	下毛毛雨
drought	干旱	dull	阴天的
fair	晴朗的;转晴的	foggy	浓雾的
freeze	(使)结冰,(使)冷冻	frosty	结霜的,严寒的
gale	大风	gloomy	阴沉的
gust of wind	阵风	hail	冰雹;下冰雹
haze	薄雾	hurricane	飓风;强热带风暴(美国)
lightning	闪电	meteorology	气象学;气象状态
mild	(气温)适中的	mist	薄雾
nasty	令人不快的;讨厌的	oppressive	闷热的
overcast	阴天的	precipitation	降水;降水量
rainfall	降雨;降雨量	rotten	坏的;恶劣的
sand storm	沙暴	scorching	灼热的
sleet	下冻雨;下雨夹雪	snowfall	降雪;降雪量
snowflake	雪花	splendid	极好的
sultry	闷热的;酷热的	sunny	阳光充足的
tempest	暴风雨;起大风暴	thunder	雷声;打雷
tornado	内陆龙卷风	typhoon	台风
warm and nice	暖洋洋的	waterspout	海上龙卷风
whirlwind	旋风	wretched	恶劣的,非常坏的

Task Procedure

1. Individually, recall local weather information about last week and fill out the following table.

Days in Last Week	Weather	Temperature		Humidity	Wind	Remarks
		Hi	Lo	(%)	(km/h)	
Sunday						

continued

Days in Last Week	Weather	Temperature		Humidity (%)	Wind (km/h)	Remarks
		Hi	Lo			
Monday						
Tuesday						
Wednesday						
Thursday						
Friday						
Saturday						

2. Show your completed table to your pair and find out if your pair has got the same information for all the days in the last week. If you cannot get an agreement on some items for a certain day, try to show your pair the evidence to support yourself or turn to others for further information.

3. Suppose you and your pair are working for a local meteorological service center. As chief forecasters, both of you are required to officially release the local weather update on a TV channel this evening. Now you need work together to prepare a written script of the weather report. Remember you should include the following besides the regular weather information:

　　a. Air Quality　Daily report on local air quality is also available in many cities. Add it to your report if it is so.

　　b. Suggestions　You may also include some ideas or suggestions for the tourists and local residents in your reporting.

4. Since this is the first time for you or your pair to be a forecaster, you need some forms of practicing. Now in your regular group, practice your weather update before you might be selected to do it before your class later on.

5. Name one of group members the official weather forecaster of your group and collectively revise the written script, focusing on both the correctness of the information and language form.

6. After your group get the previous job done, each member presents orally the most terrible weather she or he has ever encountered and then select one of your members to report her/his personal story to the class later on.

7. The table below shows the typical weather information of Beijing, Shanghai, Tianjin, Harbin, Urumchi and Shenzhen in January. Select one student in your group to read the weather report to others in the group. The listeners should jot down the information in

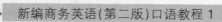

their notepad and are allowed to ask for repetition of the information if necessary.

City	Weather	Temperature		Humidity	Visibility	Wind
		Hi	Lo	(%)	(km/h)	(km/h)
Beijing	Sunny	3°	−9°	34	16	6 NW
Shanghai	overcast	12°	0°	81	3	19 ENE
Tianjin	Clear	6°	−6°	54	18	7 W
Harbin	Snow	−17°	−29°	66	8	26 NNW
Urumchi	Snow	1°	−12°	39	1	15 NE
Shenzhen	Shower	22°	14°	96	5	32 SE

NW = northwest

ENE = east northeast

NNW = north northwest

8. Listeners in the group should get prepared for the following questions and discuss in the group.

   a. Which city would you like to visit if you have a week off next January based on the weather information provided in the above table? Why?

   b. Which city would you not like to visit? Why?

   c. Introduce to your group members the climate in your hometown.

9. Class activity:

   a. Group representatives present their weather updates as forecasters before class.

   b. Group representatives present their personal stories about the most terrible weather she or he has ever experienced.

   c. Teacher may invite some students to deliver their opinions based on the information and discussion at step 8.

Unit Four

E-communication

 **Warm Up**

1. Say out Loud and Fast

1) I would like to refund this mobile phone.

2) Cell phone leads me a tough life.

3) A mobile phone has become a most sophisticated palm computer.

4) This'll be the network of all communication channels used in NATO.

5) Please keep a professional manner of speaking to communicate with our clients.

6) These five tips for online communications strategies will pump up your public-relations efforts.

7) Blogs often offer commentary on a particular subject, such as food, politics, or local news.

8) This section gives a brief overview of some of the jargon involved in e-communication.

9) Our prepaid phone cards are your best choice for long distance savings! Pay 20 dollars and talk 33 hours.

10) Marry wanted to reach her husband on his mobile phone but discovered she was out of credit.

2. Culture Tip

When you use a public telephone in a foreign country, be sure to read the directions carefully before dialing the number. In many foreign countries, as in China, a special number is assigned to each region of the country, which is called an "area code". If you know the area code and the phone number, it is usually easier and cheaper to dial the number yourself. In some foreign countries, such as in the UK and USA, you can make reverse charge or collect calls with the help of an operator, and if the person you are calling accepts your call, he will pay for the call.

Also phone companies in both UK and USA offer a credit card service, commonly called a phone card, to their customers. You get a card with an account number and a PIN (Personal Identity Number), which you can use for any phone. You pay for your calls after you have made them when the bill is sent to your home.

Dialogues

Dialogue A   A Video Conference

Recently, a monthly report from Geoffrey, Human Resource Director, has drawn Mr. White's attention. The report shows a noticeable high turnover rate in young staff members, especially in technical areas. Mr. White called an urgent video conference with following directors at different cities to discuss this issue.

Geoffrey:	*Human Resource（HR）Director from Head office in Shanghai*
Lisa:	*Public Relations（PR）Director from Beijing Branch*
Max:	*Manufacturing Department（MD）Director from Wuhan Branch*
Steve:	*Research and Development（R & D）Director from Guangzhou Branch*

Mr. White: Good afternoon, everyone. Thanks for attending the meeting at such a short notice. I have gone through the monthly reports from each department and noticed that the young employee turnover is very high in technical area. The purpose of the meeting is to identify the causes and try to find a solution to this issue.

Geoffrey: I have to admit that it's getting tougher to communicate with the young employees. The young people today are stereotyped as self-centered and concerned only with making money.

Lisa: I agree with Geoffrey. Today, young employees are less likely to work for one employer for longer period and more willing to change jobs to achieve goals set by themselves. Instead of working up the corporate ladder in the same company, new graduates prefer to build up their résumés with different employers and various positions. I am not surprised that the turnover is high in young staff in our company.

Max: I feel the same way. A generation ago, young people were committed to their employers. But now, it seems that a lot talented young technicians just flow to wherever can offer them a higher salary.

Mr. White: I understand that high turnover is getting popular with young employees. Many can't stay in the same company for more than a year or two. But young staff is a very strong support in the technical area. Steve, what do you think?

Steve: I think it differently. Today, young technicians may be less committed to one employer. But they are more committed to creation and innovation than any other previous generation.

Lisa: Absolutely true! They are better educated, grow up with technology and can cope with change and challenge.

Steve: Max, remember last month you had a new product line called "The Ultimate On-line Gaming Machine". It's actually one of our young technicians' idea. He is an on-line game player and always hears other players complain that all the computers are very slow when playing on-line games. So he has this idea of designing a computer especially for on-line gaming players.

Mr. White: Yes. I remember that. The computer has generated a lot of profit for the company. I do agree that our young technicians are very talented. That's why I am worried that we can't keep these talented people. The high turnover rate reflects that there must be something wrong with the management in the company. Any suggestion about what we can do next?

Geoffrey: I think we need to understand them before we can actually manage them. I know that they have a QQ group, on which they exchange ideas, comment on the hot news, and even plan car pooling and traveling. You can name a lot.

Mr. White: QQ?

Geoffrey: It's an Internet communication program, like MSN Messenger in US.

Mr. White: I see.

Geoffrey: I am thinking that maybe we can establish an effective communication channel in their QQ group. We post topics or questions and collect their responses.

Mr. White: Good! HR department will deal with establishing communication channel with the young staff. But if you join in their QQ group, remember, just listen, no comments on the sensitive issues!

Geoffrey: We won't.

Mr. White: Max and Steve, could you please assist Geoffrey whenever necessary as most of the young staff members are in your areas?

Max and Steve: No problem.

Mr. White: Let's give it a month to collect information. I will organize another meeting with you in a month time. Hopefully, we can come up with a solution to this problem by then.

Dialogue B   A Call to New York

Mrs. Ruth Cooper is the sales representative of Shanghai Computer Company. She is working in New York branch. Henry White wants to talk to her on the phone.

Receptionist: Shanghai Computer Company, New York Branch. This is Sarah.

Henry: Hello, Sarah, this is Henry White, from Shanghai Office. Would you please put me through to Mrs. Ruth Cooper in Sales Department?

Receptionist: Sure, can you hold the line please? (*After checking the line.*) Sorry, Mr. White. The line is busy. Do you want to leave her a message or wait?

Henry: I'd rather wait.

(*After a few minutes.*)

Ruth: Ruth Cooper speaking.

Henry: Hello, Ruth. This is Henry. How are you?

Ruth: Hi, Henry. I'm fine. I rang you this morning, but couldn't reach you on your mobile.

Henry: Sorry about that. I was in the manufacturing area. The cell phone signal is weak there.

Ruth: I just called to let you know that the Market Research Department reported a big demand of computers in South American area.

Henry: Great! We need it. The sales volume in Asia dropped by one third in the second quarter of the year. I hope the sales in South America can make up for the loss.

Ruth: People tend to buy new computers either for kids or themselves as New Year's gifts. A 20% drop in sales in the second quarter is normal, but I didn't expect so much in the Asian market this year. How come?

Henry: According to our recent customer survey, some of our computers don't perform very well while running internet-based programs, such as instant messaging applications and online games.

Ruth: We've got the similar feedback from the customers here too. That's certainly not pleasant.

Henry: No, not at all. We're hurrying our pace to develop a new model, which hopefully can come out just before the school holiday begins here. Then it can be shipped to South America before the New Year sale starts.

Ruth: Please don't hesitate to contact me if you need my help.

Henry: Thank you, Ruth. By the way, I'm going to host a video conference with the sales reps in South Asia and North America this Friday morning. We'll discuss how to promote the new model and how to open up the new market. Ruth, would you please introduce your success in the South American market at the conference? We desperately need some good news to cheer up the staff right now.

Ruth: No problem. I'll take care of it.

Henry: Thank you very much. Have a good day.

Ruth: You too. Bye, Henry.

Dialogue C   Chatting on the Internet

Late in the evening, Richard is still surfing the Internet. Suddenly, a dialogue box pops up. Isabel gets online.

Richard: Hi, Isabel.

Isabel: Richard, I'm going to Shanghai during this coming summer vacation.

Richard: Great. Will you come here alone?

Isabel: No. There are 15 students in all. Actually I take a course on Asian studies this semester. As a part of the curriculum, there is a 3-week Asian tour in the summer vacation. Professor Jack Mason is the team leader. We'll go to Hong Kong first. Shanghai is our second stop. Then move northward to Beijing, Seoul and Osaka.

Richard: How long will you stay in Shanghai?

Isabel: A week. We have a research project there on The Change and The City. Richard, will you give me some suggestion?

Richard: Let me think. (*Thinking ...*) I got one. Suzhou River is the mainstream of the city, known as the Mother River by the local people. It runs across the city, carrying on history and culture of this mysterious oriental metropolis. Many stories happened across the river. What do you think?

Isabel: That's great!

Richard: When you are here, I'll organize a boat tour on the river, together with Mom and Dad.

Isabel: Terrific! How are Mom and Dad?

Richard: They're both quite well.

Isabel: Give my best regards to them. How about your girlfriend Ying?

Richard: She's touring France and Germany.

Isabel:	Will she be with us when I'm in Shanghai?
Richard:	Yes, she will be back early next month.
Isabel:	I can't wait to meet her.
Richard:	I guarantee you'll like her. She's a sweet girl. Have you booked the plane tickets yet?
Isabel:	Yes. Let me check it. It's MU9021, arrives at 9 a.m., local time, on the 10th of July.
Richard:	There are two airports in Shanghai, Pudong International Airport and Hongqiao Airport. Do you know which one you're landing?
Isabel:	Sorry, I have no idea.
Richard:	Don't worry. I'll check it and meet you at the airport.
Isabel:	OK. See you then.
Richard:	Take care of yourself. I'll get off-line. Bye.

Dialogue D   Romance via Micro-blogging

It's 9 p.m. on Monday night. Richard and Ying are talking on the cell phone.

Richard:	Honey, how was your day?
Ying:	It was a long day. We were rehearsing a new ballet play. I had to learn a lot of new movements. That was a bit of challenge and made me practicing all day.
Richard:	Don't get yourself hurt.
Ying:	You're telling me!
Richard:	What?
Ying:	I mean I will take care of myself.
Richard:	Ying, are you still there? I can't hear you. The signal is poor. Let's hang up. I'll call you right back.
	(*A minute later, they are connected again.*)
Richard:	Here we go. I heard a story today.
Ying:	About what?
Richard:	About micro-blog. A man posted a message on his micro-blog that he lost his briefcase in the subway. A subway staff happened to read the message, and he replied to that man that his briefcase was in the Lost and Found of the subway station.
Ying:	It's unbelievable! Richard, I got a story about micro-blog, too.
Richard:	I'm all ears.
Ying:	A young man and a girl got to know each other on micro-blog. They fell

in love, and after one year's dating, the young man decided to propose to the girl.

Richard: Did the girl say yes?

Ying: The girl said "since we got acquainted through micro-blog, you must post this proposal on your micro-blog. If the message is read and relayed by one thousand people, I'll say yes." Guess what?

Richard: Come on, I can't wait!

Ying: It turned out that the message was answered by fifty thousand people!

Richard: Wow, that's cool!

Ying: Isn't that romantic!

Richard: Hey, wait! Honey, are you suggesting something?

Ying: (*Giggling on the other end of the phone*.) I didn't say anything!

Notes

1.	video conference	视频会议
2.	turnover rate	员工流动率, 跳槽比例
3.	urgent	紧急的
4.	Human Resource (HR)	人力资源部
5.	Public Relations (PR)	公共关系部
6.	Manufacturing Department (MD)	生产部
7.	Research and Development (R & D)	研发部
8.	stereotyped	把……模式化
9.	self-centered	以自我为中心的
10.	the sensitive issues	敏感话题
11.	instant messaging application	(网上)即时通讯应用程序
12.	online game	在线游戏
13.	sales representative	销售代表
14.	New York branch	纽约分公司
15.	put through	(电话)接通
16.	couldn't reach you on your mobile	你手机无法接通
17.	cell phone signal	手机信号
18.	make up for the loss	弥补损失
19.	the second quarter of the year	第二季度
20.	How come?	怎么会这样?
21.	hurry our pace	加紧步伐
22.	sales reps (= sales representative)	销售代表

23. cheer up	鼓舞
24. surfing the Internet	上网
25. a dialogue box pops up	跳出一个对话框
26. curriculum	课程计划
27. 3-week Asian tour	为期3周的亚洲之旅
28. Seoul	首尔(韩国首都)
29. Osaka	大阪(日本)
30. research project	科研项目
31. oriental metropolis	东方大都市
32. terrific	太棒了
33. via micro-blogging	通过微博交流
34. How was your day?	你今天过得怎么样?
35. It was a long day.	今天可累坏了。
36. You're telling me!	还用你说!
37. hang up	挂电话
38. call back	回电(话)
39. Here we go.	现在好啦!
40. relay	转发
41. I'm all ears.	我洗耳恭听。
42. giggle	咯咯地笑

 Functional Expressions

Speaking to Someone on the Phone

1. Hello, is this the Accounting Department? I'd like to speak to Mrs. Wright.
2. Is Mr. Bettelheim there?
3. Is Mrs. White in?
4. May I speak to Mr. Andrews, please?

Getting Someone Else to Answer the Phone

1. Dr. Leemann, you are wanted on the phone.
2. Hold on, please.
3. Just a moment, please.
4. Just hold the line for a second, please.
5. Miss Kelly wants to speak to you on the phone.
6. Mr. Young is on the line, Shellie.

7. Somebody's asking for you on the phone.

8. Someone wants you on the phone, honey.

9. There is a phone call for you, Jimmy.

Answering the Phone

1. Hello, this is Bill.

2. Hi, Jerry speaking.

3. I can't make out what you are saying. Speak as loud as you can, please.

4. I'll ask her to give you a ring as soon as she comes back?

5. Jennifer is taking a shower now. Would you like to have her call you back?

6. Mark is on his vacation. Could you leave your name?

7. Mrs. Amasova is at a meeting. Would you like to leave a message?

8. My mom is out shopping. Do you want her to return your call when she is back?

9. Pardon? It's not clear. Could you speak a little louder?

10. Please speak as loud as possible.

11. Put the receiver closer to your mouth, please.

12. She is not in right now. Would you like to leave your telephone number?

13. Sorry, I can't hear you clearly. Speak louder, please.

14. Vanessa, is that you calling?

15. Who's speaking?

16. Who's this speaking?

17. Who's this?

18. Yes, speaking.

19. You must have dialed some other number.

20. You must have dialed the wrong number.

Speaking to the Operator

1. I'd like to make a long-distance call at 403 - 62378201, please.

2. Operator, I want to make a reverse charge call to Beijing, 010 - 2588588, extension 666.

3. Please put me through to Mrs. Carroll.

4. Yes, I need to put a person-to-person call, Mr. Brown at 9 - 7210639.

Answering from the Operator

1. Mr. Hilton, the line is engaged at the moment.

2. Sir, you are through.

3. Sorry, nobody is answering.

4. The line is busy.

5. The number is busy, Ms. Qian.

 Communicative Task

Making a Phone Call from Campus

Types of Task: pair, group.

Functions Practiced: starting a phone conversation, checking someone has understood you, identifying formal and informal speech, asking for advice.

Pre-task

1. Try to recall as much as possible the last real telephone call you made in Chinese and in your real life.

2. Write down the contents of your last real telephone call on a piece of paper and translate it into English. The English version should be as true as possible to the original in Chinese. You should underline in the English version any problems you have had in translating particular words or phrases.

3. Then work with your pair and try to improve on the accuracy of both of your English versions. When you are talking about the improvements, try to use sentences like "Would you tell me how to ...?", "Do you think it is right to ...?" or "Could you write ... for me?" to make yourself in a proper way to ask for help from others.

4. Now you write down on a piece of paper some real telephone numbers you can remember in your mind or some imaginary ones. If it is too embarrassing for you to give off the real phone numbers, make up some for yourself.

5. The phone list should include name, company, social identity, relationship to you, etc.

6. Exchange the phone lists with your pair.

7. If you have no idea as to how to start out a conversation on telephone, refer to this Unit or see the examples given bellow.

Some possible ways to start out conversations on phone:

Example 1

Student A: (makes a ringing tone)

Student B: (answers) *Hello*.

Student A: (checks the number) *Hello, is that 62562799?*

Student B: (confirms) *Yes*.

Student A: (asks for B by name) *Can I speak to Robin please?*

Student B: (continues according to the telephone number given) *Robin doesn't live here any more.*

. . .

Example 2

Student A: (makes a ringing tone)

Student B: *Hello.*

Student A: *May I speak to David, please?*

Student B: *Speaking.*

. . .

Example 3

Student A: (makes a ringing tone)

Student B: (answers) *Royal Fashion Company, may I help you?*

Student A: *I'd like to have a word with Sysilia, Sysilia Anderson.*

Student B: *Mrs. Anderson is out of town at the moment, but I'm her secretary. Can I take a message?*

. . .

Task Procedure

1. Now you and your pair sit back to back. Take turns to select two or three phone numbers from your pair's phone list to make phone calls via an imaginary telephone line.

2. Use a recorder for this part to record your telephone conversations, if possible.

3. Play back the recording and make a transcript of your phone calls. Do some corrections if necessary.

4. In your group, offer your tape transcript to the other group members.

5. Read carefully the other's transcripts and pick up at least three sentences in the transcripts and rewrite them in your own way without changing the meanings.

6. Take turns in the group to discuss the appropriateness of the language forms in relation to their meanings and occasions.

7. Now read through your fellow student's telephone conversations again and try to rate the conversations according to the criteria of formality: formal, less formal and informal. Copy some sentences that you believe they are well organized and best expressed and might be useful in your future phone calls or daily life.

Unit Five

Requests and Offers

 **Warm Up**

1. Say out Loud and Fast

1) Henry White has just refused a strange request from a businessman.

2) Sophia at my request told him the status of our negotiations.

3) We granted your request to lower the prices of our products.

4) You're requested to furnish us with two copies of the quotes.

5) Could we request the honor of your presence at our opening ceremony?

6) At your request, we now hold this offer firm till 31 July.

7) He offered to see me through college.

8) The firm offer we emailed you on Monday remains open for the next 10 days.

9) Our community college offers a two-year associate degree.

10) The football club tried to tempt the player with offers of money.

2. Culture Tip

When you ask for something or ask someone to do something, it is important to be polite. If you think someone might refuse your request, you may ask the question in a way that the refusal won't cause embarrassment for both of you. However, when you are offering something to a Westerner, remember it is quite important to learn the way they accept or turn down your offers. Generally speaking, when a Briton or an American says "no" to your offering, he means it. Any persistence in your offering could be regarded as either ignorance or rudeness.

In return if a Westerner offers you something, like a seat, he may do so only once. So if you feel you want it, say "Thank you" or "You're so kind" and take his offer. If you are at a

Westerner's home and you need a drink or the toilet or you need some fresh air you can ask politely and they won't be offended.

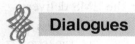 **Dialogues**

Dialogue A   Driving in Shanghai

Henry White rings Shanghai Municipal Department of Vehicles (SMDV) and wants to know the information on driver license in Shanghai. Haidong Chen in SMDV is answering the phone.

Haidong: Good afternoon, welcome to Shanghai Municipal Department of Vehicles (SMDV). This is Haidong Chen speaking. How may I help you?

Henry: Hi, my name is Henry White. I'm from the United States and now working in Shanghai. I'd like to get a driver license in Shanghai. Could you please give me some information about this?

Haidong: Welcome to Shanghai, Mr. White. I am happy to help you with the information to obtain your license. Do you have a valid US driver license?

Henry: Yes, I have a driver license, and it was issued by the City of New York. I wonder if my license is acceptable to drive in Shanghai.

Haidong: Sorry, Mr. White. Unfortunately your US driver license is not valid in China. But it will help you to get your Chinese driver license.

Henry: Will it? You mean I can get my license right now?

Haidong: No, not exactly. To obtain a Shanghai driver license, you must pass a written test and a road test. In your case, you don't need to take the road test, but you will need to pass the written test. The written test is mandatory for everyone with no exception.

Henry: A written test? I guess the written test must have something to do with the traffic regulations.

Haidong: You are right, Mr. White. The written test is about the traffic regulations and general driving knowledge in Shanghai, such as recognition and reaction to other vehicles, pedestrians and cyclists.

Henry: I understand. Every country has its own road rules which are certainly different.

Haidong: That's right. To prepare for your test, you need to study a handbook issued by SMDV which contains important road safety and road law information that will prepare you for safe driving.

Henry:	Yes, I need it, of course. Where can I get it? Bookstore?
Haidong:	No, it is available only at this department. You can come to the office to buy it. Alternatively, you may purchase it from our Online Bookshop and pay online. 28RMB for the handbook plus 25RMB for the EMS delivery.
Henry:	I prefer to purchase it online. Could you tell me your website address?
Haidong:	I will send the Online Bookshop address to your mobile. Is 1304970157 your number?
Henry:	Yes.
Haidong:	You'll get the message in a minute. What else can I do for you, Mr. White?
Henry:	Yes, one more thing. Where and when can I sit the written test?
Haidong:	You can do the test in one of our Test Centers. But you need to make an appointment with us in advance. Appointment can be made online, by calling us or visiting our office. Our office opens from 8 a.m. to 4 p.m., Monday to Friday. The testing fee is 100RMB; both cash and credit card are acceptable.
Henry:	OK. Do I need to bring anything with me when I sit the written test?
Haidong:	You need to bring your current passport, your US driver license, a reference letter from your employer which states your employment status and your current home address.
Henry:	OK. Also can I choose to sit the written test in English?
Haidong:	Yes you can. There are some sample questions on our website you can practice.
Henry:	Thank you, Mr. Chen. I do appreciate your help.
Haidong:	You are welcome. Enjoy the rest of the day.

Dialogue B   Driving Test

After lunch, Sophia is washing the dishes in the kitchen, while Henry gives up his usual daily after-meal-walking and is reading the driver's handbook in the study room. Suddenly Henry puts down the handbook, and walks into the kitchen.

Henry:	Honey, may I ask you a favor?
Sophia:	Sure, what is it?
Henry:	I'm preparing for the written driving test. But, you know, there are 400 some questions in the driver's handbook and next Tuesday morning I'm supposed to take the test.
Sophia:	That's a lot. But do you have to know all the answers? How many questions

are there in a test?

Henry: One hundred. To pass the test, I have to answer 90 questions correctly.

Sophia: Well, it's pretty hard, isn't it? I don't think you can pass it next Tuesday. Only three days left.

Henry: I must and I can't afford the time. I'll go to Guangzhou in two weeks and lots of things have to be done before I'm leaving. Besides, I'm the first one in the company to take the driving test and they all know I'll take the test next Tuesday.

Sophia: Among all the staff from the United States?

Henry: All the staff from all over the world, except China, of course. I must memories all the questions and answers before sitting in the test room. Trust me I can pass it. My IQ is 125 and my memory is still working very well.

Sophia: Yes, yes, Honey. You'll remember all the answers, I believe.

Henry: Thank you for your encouragement.

Sophia: I wish I could be with you and help you. I know your learning style. Your best way to learn is to have someone to study with you.

Henry: And plus a discussion with someone. It enhances learning. I've already read all the chapters in the handbook during the lunch break in the past three days as soon as I got the handbook and now the chance for me to pass is 50 percent after I took ten practice tests online. I want to make sure I know all the answers before next Tuesday.

Sophia: Good for you. They have the online tests. Why don't you continue to take the online practice tests?

Henry: Well, it wasted me too much time.

Sophia: Why? Did you play games while taking the tests as you had done it before in the university?

Henry: Oh, give me a break. I quit playing online games ever since I was with this computer company. I am now making computers and games, not playing.

Sophia: OK. And then continue to take the online practice tests, which will certainly help you with the comprehension of the road rules.

Henry: I said it wasted me too much time. The first three tests were fine. However, I found at least half of the questions were repeated from the third one on. In the tenth test I found at least 90% questions were repeated ones. I already know the answers.

Sophia: Now I understand why you said it wasted you too much time. Is it supposed to be just some sample questions for you to familiar with the test?

Henry: Yes, I guess so.

Sophia：	Well，stop complaining! I guess the programmer didn't include all 400 questions in the online tests for obvious reasons.
Henry：	I would have fired him if he were the employee of my company.
Sophia：	Still complaining!
Henry：	No, I didn't. I just hate to do, again and again, the questions I already know the answers.
Sophia：	Look, Henry. I'd like to help you right now, but I made an appointment to do my hair at two this afternoon. I have to run now. I'll be back at five or so. Shall we review all the new questions together after supper?
Henry：	Sorry, I didn't know it. Go ahead. I will do some questions by myself and …
Richard：	Hi, I am back.
Henry：	Hi, are you free this afternoon?
Richard：	Yes. What can I do for you, Sir? Some routine chores on Saturday afternoon, like cleaning or washing?
Henry：	Surely you can do something for me. But not the usual Saturday chores, instead, something academic.
Richard：	Academic? I like doing something academic.
Sophia：	What your father really means is to help him to go over the questions for his driving test. See you. I have to run. Do my hair.
Richard：	See you, Mum. (*Turn to Harry*.) Questions for driving test? You call them academic?
Henry：	Yes. Anything done in the study room is academic. Come on, Richard. I am waiting for you in the study room.
Richard：	OK, I'll be with you in a minute. (*In low voice*.) I prefer something physical on Saturday afternoon, though.

Dialogue C   Driving the Aussie Way

A group of Richard's colleagues will be transferred to Melbourne to set up a new trading office for the company. While the board of directors is busy with this new office setting up, the first thing the group members are doing is to ask Richard to give them some advice on driving. Now a briefing goes on in a seminar room. Sitting and listening to Richard's talk are Yunsheng, Donna, Jianhua, Dashan and Heping, the group leader.

Richard：	I've talked about driving customs and laws in general based on the fact that Australian people drive on the left-hand side of the road, which might give you some troubles, because you all are used to driving on the right-hand

side of the road in Shanghai. To test your understanding of my lecture on Driving the Aussie Way, now I will ask you some questions.

Yunsheng: Good teaching methodology. You're a wonderful teacher, Richard.

Donna: I'm a slow learner. I need more time to review the notes, I'm afraid.

Jianhua: Come on, Donna. Better to answer questions now. This is the best way to review. I'm ready, Richard.

Dashan: I'm ready too.

Heping: Don't be panic, Donna. We are all with you.

Richard: OK, everyone. Remember I said when driving in Australia, it was important to park properly to avoid getting a ticket? Now we start with the parking rules. What are the rules for parking? Anyone wants to answer this question?

Dashan: Always watch for signs. We can park off-streets where no NO STANDING, NO PARKING, or other restrictions apply. And ...

Yunsheng: We can also park at carparks or parking stations, usually at an hourly rate. I remember there is one more rule about the parking, but ...

Jianhua: I know. The last one is you can park where there are parking meters so long as you feed them with the right money, and don't overstay.

Richard: Well done. What vehicles are allowed to park in the places with the sign of LOADING AND UNLOADING ZONE?

Jianhua: If you're driving a truck, van or wagon, you're allowed to park here if you're delivering or picking up some sort of cargo.

Richard: Is that all?

Heping: No. A passenger car is also allowed only if it is for delivering.

Richard: Good. Now the next question. What is the speed limit in a built-up residential area and what is it on country roads.

Donna: The speed limit in a built-up residential area is 60 kilometers per hour. The speed limit on country roads is 80. I am not quite sure about it.

Richard: Correct for the speed limit in a built-up residential area. But ...

Yunsheng: The speed limit on country roads is 100. I also remember that you mentioned we can go at 100 even if there is no sign on country roads, unless speed limit other than 100 is indicated.

Richard: Excellent. Now the questions about the roundabouts which are the typical road facilities in Australia. What are the general rules about the roundabouts?

Heping: Traffic in a roundabout flows in a clockwise direction. I must give way to all vehicles on my right side if we reach the roundabout at the same time. In a two-lane roundabout, In a ... Sorry, I forget the rest.

Yunsheng: In a two-lane roundabout，we must keep to the left lane if we're turning left or going straight ahead. Besides，we should keep to the right lane if we're turning right. We can also use the right lane in a two-lane roundabout if we're going straight ahead.

Heping: The most important is to use the correct signal to exit from a roundabout. The rules are：use the left-turn signal for a left turn，the right-turn signal for a right turn. If we're turning right and are on the right lane，we must switch on our left-turn signal when exiting.

Donna: What a remarkable memory!

Richard: Great，Heping. I know you're also an excellent driver. Now，everyone，the last question. There is a path across the road. You are facing a "Give Way" sign. Who must you give way to，bicyclist or pedestrians?

Donna: I remember this，both of them，you said that，right?

Richard: Good job，Donna. Remember both bicycles and pedestrians have the priority and the right of road，unless there is a sign to allow the drivers to go first.

Jianhua: We have a similar rule here. Drivers must respect pedestrians. Yeh，in any case life is most important.

Richard: Well，this comes to the end of my briefing on Driving the Aussie Way. Thank you for your attendance.

Heping: Thank you very much，Richard. That is a marvelous lecture，indeed. On behalf of all members of the group，I invite you to have dinner with us. At the Chinese restaurant across the street. 6 p. m. I know you like Chinese food.

Richard: Yes，thank you for offering me my favorite food.

Dialogue D   Hook Turn

Henry White is sitting in the living room and thinking about the phone call from Richard. Richard told that he was presenting a briefing on driving in Australia for his colleagues and would be home around ten o'clock. Henry looks a bit uneasy in the sofa and seems anxious to know what Richard was talking about on this topic.

Henry: How about your lecture of Driving the Aussie Way?

Richard: It was perfect. My colleagues were happy and grateful. Look，this is the present from them，a bottle of French wine plus a splendid dinner.

Henry: But you've never been to Australia，not to mention driving in any place in Australia.

Richard: Well，one doesn't have to experience everything personally. To me driving is just a piece of cake. I told them every bit of all Jason told me: Being a leftist while driving in Australia, driving on the left-hand side of the road, cautions when approaching to roundabouts, speed limits in various areas. Of course, the skills to make sure to go into the left-hand side of the road when turning left or right, instead of to the right as they are used to. With my experience in the States and the information from Jason, their safety in Australia is guaranteed.

Henry: Did you tell them the hook turn in Melbourne?

Richard: Hook turn? What is it? Jason didn't say a word of it.

Henry: Of course not. He lives in Brisbane. Brisbane doesn't contain hook turn intersections. A hook turn is a traffic-control mechanism where cars that would normally have to turn across oncoming traffic are made to turn across all lanes of traffic instead.

Richard: Why do they have this hook turn?

Henry: Because there are trams in Melbourne. Hook turns are relatively rare in the world, but can be used to improve the flow of traffic and to keep the middle of the road free for trams.

Richard: So they use this traffic-control mechanism to give way to trams. But is it weird? It is also confusing to drivers.

Henry: It is weird. If your colleagues are new to hook turns, it can be both confusing and exasperating, and they are also likely to miss the right turn if they caught in the wrong lane.

Richard: This rule will give my colleagues extra trouble, I'm sure.

Henry: Right. Tell your colleagues to watch out for the "hook turn" signs and be prepared to turn right from the leftmost lane.

Richard: The experience tells me it is an often impossible task to move quickly to the leftmost lane when the traffic is heavy.

Henry: So be prepared in advance. Melbourne's Central Business District contains 19 hook turn intersections, with others scattered throughout the inner city area. Generally, hook turns must be made when turning right and you're sharing the road with tramlines to your immediate right. There must be a hook turn sign just ahead of you at the intersection.

Richard: Then the best way for my colleagues to drive safely is to avoid entering the streets with tramlines. I will tell them tomorrow that if they do enter those streets try to move as soon as possible to the leftmost lane. I will find the details online to mark on a map with all hook turn intersections in Melbourne tonight.

Henry: Sure. That's what you have to do to make your lecture a true perfect one.

Notes

1.	embarrassment	尴尬
2.	turn down	拒绝
3.	persistence	坚持
4.	either ignorance or rudeness	不是无知就是粗鲁
5.	in return	以同样的思维方式(接受你的答复)
6.	won't be offended	不会有被冒犯的感受
7.	Shanghai Municipal Department of Vehicles	上海市车辆管理处
8.	valid US driver license	有效的美国驾驶证
9.	road test	路考
10.	mandatory	强制的;必需的
11.	traffic regulations	交通规则
12.	pedestrian	行人
13.	25RMB for the EMS delivery	人民币 25 元的中国邮政速递费
14.	sit the written test	参加笔试
15.	I can't afford the time.	时间上,我承受不起。
16.	staff	员工
17.	IQ	智商
18.	learning style	学习风格
19.	enhance learning	增强学习效果
20.	practice tests online	在线模拟测试
21.	give me a break	得了吧,饶了我吧
22.	Well,stop complaining!	好了,别抱怨了!
23.	for obvious reasons	出于明显的原因
24.	I would have fired him.	我真想把他解雇了。
25.	do my hair	做头发,烫头发
26.	I have to run now.	我得赶紧去了。
27.	routine chores	日常家务
28.	something academic	与学术相关的活动
29.	Aussie(Australian)	澳大利亚
30.	be transferred to Melbourne	调去墨尔本工作
31.	trading office	贸易公司办事处
32.	the board of directors	董事会
33.	seminar room	研讨会会议室
34.	a briefing	情况介绍会
35.	teaching methodology	教学法,教学方法

36. Don't be panic. We are all with you.	别害怕,有我们呢。
37. to avoid getting a ticket	免得吃罚单
38. off-streets	非主要街道,背街小巷
39. NO STANDING	禁止车辆停留
40. at an hourly rate	以小时计算(停车时间)
41. don't overstay	不要超时停车
42. ute	家用轿车式小货车(类似皮卡)
43. a built-up residential area	居民区,道路两旁有建筑物的区域
44. roundabout	环状交叉路口,转盘道
45. a clockwise direction	顺时针方向
46. left-turn signal	左转弯信号
47. a "Give Way" sign	一个"让路"标志(牌子)
48. the right of road	路权
49. in any case	在任何情况下
50. hook turn	弯钩状大转弯
51. a bit uneasy	有点坐立不安(烦躁)
52. a splendid dinner	一顿丰盛的晚餐
53. a piece of cake	容易的事
54. be guaranteed	有保障的
55. oncoming traffic	迎面而来的车流
56. tram	有轨电车
57. weird	古怪的,不可思议的
58. confusing and exasperating	令人困惑、恼怒的
59. intersection	路口
60. tramlines	有轨电车轨道线

 Functional Expressions

Making a Request

1. Any chance of using your telephone?
2. Can you give me a lift?
3. Could you possibly put me up for the night?
4. Could you spare me some ink, please?
5. Do you mind if I use your pen for a moment please?
6. Give me something to drink, will you please?
7. I'd appreciate it if you could stop smoking, please.

8. I'm sorry to trouble you，but could you phone the police?

9. May I ask you a favor?

10. Mind typing it for me?

11. Will you be able to get this done by Tuesday?

12. Would you mind changing this ten-yuan note for me，please?

Making a Negative Response to a Request

1. I'd like to say yes，but that's just impossible.

2. I'd like to help you，but I don't have any change on me.

3. I'd rather not if you don't mind.

4. I'd really like to，but I don't know if I should.

5. I'd really like to help you out，but I'm broke myself.

6. I'm sorry，but I'm using it right now.

7. Sorry，it can't be done.

8. Sorry，old chaps，nothing doing.

Offering Something

1. A bottle of French wine for you.

2. A glass of wine?

3. Can I offer you a little gift?

4. Could I offer you something to read?

5. Fancy some caviar? We can share this can.

6. Help yourself to this apple pie.

7. Here's a little token of my affection.

8. Please take it.

9. This is a small something for you. I hope you like it.

10. What can I get you?

11. What would you say to a night out?

12. Which one would you like to take?

13. Why don't you have some chocolate?

14. Won't you have a drink?

15. Would you care for a coke?

16. Would you like some orange?

17. You like mushrooms? I can offer you some, if you like.

Accepting an Offer of Something

1. Great.

2. I can think of nothing better.

3. I'd be so pleased if you would.

4. I'd like it very much, please.

5. I'd love some.

6. If you would, please.

7. It's exactly what I wanted.

8. It's just lovely.

9. Oh, please. Thanks a lot.

10. Thank you so much, but you really shouldn't have done that.

11. That would be a great help.

12. That would be very nice.

13. That's just what I wanted. Thank you.

14. With pleasure.

15. You bet.

Declining an Offer of Something

1. I won't, thanks.

2. If it's all the same to you, I won't.

3. No, thank you.

4. No, thanks.

5. Not for me, thank you.

6. Not this time, thanks.

7. Thanks all the same, but I won't.

8. That's very kind, but I won't.

 Communicative Task

The Priorities of Buying a New Home

Types of Task: group, class.

Functions Practiced: stating your idea, accepting other's idea, asking somebody what he prefers, stating what you prefer.

Pre-task

1. The list below is some of the common priorities that most people keep in their minds when they are going to buy a new home.

2. Tick off three of them in the list you think they are your top priorities when you are going to buy a new home, or you may add three more priorities you believe they are most important to your life.

3. Under the heading "Reasons" guess and write down why you and some people consider a particular item as their top priority.

Common Priorities for Buying a Home

Priorities for buying a home	Reasons
near the countryside	
facing south	
full of natural light	
a house, not an apartment	
with nice views	
outside of downtown	
not in a rough neighborhood	
in the city center	
with amenities nearby	

4. Go around the classroom and find some others who got the same priorities as yours. With them form a new group (about 6 students), name your new group in a unique way, for example, Facing-south Group, indicating the most remarkable feature of your priorities.

5. **OR**: If you are an assertive person and you want to test your leadership you are allowed in this task to call out in the class to recruit your classmates with the same interests into your group by shouting, for instance, "My priority is ... Any one who is interested in this priority join my group, please.", or " ... are my priorities of buying a new home. Welcome to my group, if you like to own a home like this."

Task Procedure

1. In your new group, first get your group name done. You can even design a logo for your new group to distinguish yourself.

2. Draw the logo with your group name on a big label and put it on your group's desk.

3. Discuss the reasons you just wrote in the above table with your new group members and guess why some people are in favor of a particular criterion. Later on your teacher might ask you this question. Get yourself prepared now.

4. In your group decide on three top priorities all your group members agreed with.

5. Make a new table like the one above and write down your three priorities.

6. Discuss and copy the reasons of your choices in the table. Later on, your group

representative will be asked to report them to your class. Select your group representative and your deputy group representative after your finish the discussion.

7. Now comes the reporting-to-class time. Wait until your teacher invites your group to offer your choice and reasons. Your group representative will report, on behalf of your whole group, the opinions on Three Priorities to Buy a New Home to the class.

8. If your group representative missed some points of your group discussion, the deputy group representative can have another opportunity to add them.

9. While listening to the presentations from other groups, you should rate, in your own notepad, each item in your own table from "the most important (MI)" to "the least important (LI)".

10. At the end of each group's presentation, you are welcome to offer your comments in favor or against the concerned groups by raising your hand first.

Unit Six

Advice and Suggestion

 Warm Up

1. Say out Loud and Fast

1) That girl is a law to herself; she never asks advice of others.

2) Thank you very much for your advice; I'll chew it over this evening.

3) He is very stubborn, and all your advice will amount to nothing.

4) You need to be discreet in giving advice, humble in accepting it.

5) Don't offer advice to those who are more experienced than you are.

6) There were 16 votes in favor of my suggestion, and 15 against.

7) The corners of her mouth suggested the least trace of irony.

8) Advice is like a drug in the market and the supply always exceeds the demand.

9) All this is not to suggest that forgetfulness doesn't come at a price.

10) It is advisable to check the instrument by frequent calibration.

2. Culture Tip

Giving advice or suggestions is quite difficult. There is a risk of sounding too forward or authoritative, especially if that person is of a higher status or it is about a sensitive issue. Generally speaking, avoid the use of "You had better ..." or any other structures that are commonly for strong advice, e.g. "I think you should ..." because these structures are used to suggest the listener has done something wrong. Use structures that give the listener the option of declining or answering your advice or suggestion, e.g. "Perhaps you could ...", "How about ..." or "Couldn't you try ...?"

The tone of your voice is also important. There are several factors to consider — the volume, texture, speed, and pitch of your voice, as well as your facial expression and body posture. When giving advice the volume of your voice should be somewhat lower than normal, the texture should be soft, the speed normal, and the pitch high. You should sound understanding, normal and open to discussion.

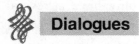 **Dialogues**

Dialogue A   High Turnover

Mr. White organized a meeting with four directors to talk about the issue of high turnover in young employees. Before the meeting, Geoffrey has forwarded a copy of the collected data to each director in e-mail.

Henry:	Good morning, everyone. Thanks for coming to the meeting. This is to follow up the meeting we had a month ago about the high turnover in young employees. Geoffrey has presented you the data collected. Now what do you think?
Max:	Geoffrey, you've done a really good job. This report has changed my view to some of my young staff members. I thought they were lazy because a lot times, I can see them doing nothing in the production line. Actually, they just work as hard as everyone else, sometimes performing their jobs more efficiently.
Henry:	Are you suggesting that we need to review the current manufacturing processes to make sure that all available resources have been fully taken advantage of?
Max:	Yes, that's what I am thinking. I will review the current process and reorganize the resources available to make sure that the use of the resources is optimized.
Steve:	The report shows that these young workers like to work collaboratively. It is contradictory to the traditional perception of "self-centered". Maybe we can set up a discussion group allowing them freedom of expression. So they can brainstorm for problem solving with different approaches. I think it will improve the productivity in my department.
Henry:	Very good!
Geoffrey:	There is a trust issue as well. In the QQ group, they complain that the management doesn't trust their ability to complete the work.
Max:	Well, I have started observing my young staff since the last meeting. I am surprised that some of them can work independently without

	supervision. It seems that we should put more trust in them.
Steve:	Yes, similar stories happened in my team. When I am away, the team supervisors take the leadership. All the team members complete their work in time with high quality standard.
Lisa:	Can I suggest a reward system? Currently, we only have a reward program running mainly in Sales area. But after reading the report I think we need a reward system in technical and production areas as well.
Geoffrey:	I agree. Staff members who contributed most should be recognized and rewarded for their well-done jobs. This will make them feel worthwhile of working for the company.
Henry:	Reward system definitely can cheer staff up. But we need to be very careful about the rewards and performance criteria. It must be transparent and fair. Geoffrey, could you please work with Max and Steve to draft a reward program plan?
Max & Steve:	No problem.
Henry:	Lisa, could you please prepare a communication note to be sent out to every staff member? Please make sure that everyone in the company gets the right message.
Lisa:	No worries. I will get things organized and send the message out.
Henry:	Thanks a lot everyone for your valuable contribution. I am confident that we can keep talented staff with us. Last but not the least, I would like to suggest that we, in management level, listen more rather than command more our staff members.

Dialogue B　Home Renovation Ideas

Mr. and Mrs. White are going to renovate their home. They are talking about different ideas and plans with their son, Richard.

Henry:	Renovating house is really a tough job! It requires a lot of energy and lots of money.
Sophia:	Don't lose heart, my darling. We are just talking about it at the moment and haven't started anything yet. I think it won't take us more than six months to do it.
Richard:	How about painting the walls of the sitting room yellow?
Henry:	Your suggestion is not bad, but the ceiling is yellow. I don't think the walls should be painted yellow as well. They should be light red or light blue.

Sophia:	I like the light red color.
Henry:	The lady's touch. We'll have the walls painted light red. Richard, will you help us to write it down?
Richard:	OK. What do you think of putting a safety lock on the door?
Sophia:	The front door or the back one?
Richard:	On the front door.
Henry:	That's not a bad idea, yet I doubt if it's necessary since the old lock is still working well.
Sophia:	I agree with you, my dear. We'd better save money. Don't change anything that can be used for the time being.
Richard:	What about getting a larger letter box? I think the old one is too small.
Henry:	We've talked about that on the phone last week. I'm for it and the larger, the better, I think.
Sophia:	Why?
Henry:	A larger one can hold bigger letters and more letters in general. Richard and I get a lot of mail every day.
Sophia:	So do I, I suppose.
Henry:	What else do you have in mind?
Sophia:	I'd like to redo the laundry. I want to put a new 5-tier shelf and replace the washing machine with a new 5 star energy-saving one.
Henry:	You are the queen.
Richard:	Speak of energy saving, I recommend the best of the best for a modern family — a solar hot water system.
Sophia:	Tell me more about it.
Richard:	Instead of using gas or electricity to heat up the water, it uses the energy from the sun. It's clean, safe, and free. It leaves no carbon footprint and it's good to the environment. Most importantly, it saves money on your bill.
Sophia:	That sounds wonderful. Then we should get one of this. What you say, Henry?
Henry:	It is a big complex system. You need a plumber to set it up and reconnect all the pipes in the laundry, kitchen, and bathrooms. My suggestion would be ... uh ... do more research before making any decisions.
Sophia:	No more research please. We'd better get the ball rolling immediately.
Richard:	Mom, leave this to me and Dad. We'll find a good solution to suit our needs in couple of days.
Sophia:	OK. That's something you boys are good at. Oh, it's about time for dinner. We'll talk about more ideas later.

Dialogue C   Product Demo

Shanghai Computer Company will host a new product demonstration. Mr. White is in charge of the project. He is discussing with his colleagues, Dongbao Wang from Testing Department and James Liu from Marketing Department, about it in a meeting room.

Henry:	Today we're going to discuss the product demonstration. I'd like to hear your suggestions. First, the location. Where do you suggest we hold it?
Dongbao:	How about the main function room? It's large enough to hold 180 people and 8 stands. We had it there last year.
Henry:	What do you think, Mr. Liu?
James:	Couldn't agree more.
Henry:	But I think we need some place bigger, because about 120 people from SME sector, 69 from education sector, 42 from government and 18 from media, have already confirmed to come so far. And more will come, I believe.
James:	Then we can add those two smaller function rooms as well.
Dongbao:	Yes. That's a good idea and won't make our guests feel too crowed.
Henry:	OK. It's settled. Second, the layout.
Dongbao:	Because we are now using three function rooms, we'd better to divide the demonstration into three main areas, the Business Computing, the Mobile Computing, and the Home Computing.
James:	Then no place to show our latest software to the audience.
Dongbao:	What if we put the software in each of the function room, together with our latest hardware?
Henry:	Brilliant idea. We can show our guests both the software and hardware at the same time. And let them see how strong our development team is. This is very different to what we had last year. I'm sure this will surprise all the guests and ensure we will have very good media coverage.
Dongbao:	Thank you very much, Mr. White.
Henry:	Good. Now the third one, the settings. What do you think?
James:	We can put our official slogan, "Shanghai Computer Company — Strive For Excellence", above the main entrance of the main function room.
Dongbao:	That's a good idea. How about we ask someone to paint a symbolic background with some famous landmark architectures to indicate our dedication to the local community?
Henry:	Good ideas. My suggestion is that we take a lot of pictures and make some models of selected landmark architectures. We should also display all of our finished products, both the old ones and the new ones, to show

our long history in the business.

James:	Great. I like your idea. Also do you think we should put some fresh flowers and green plants across the room?
Henry:	Not bad idea. I'll diarize it and discuss more details with you later. And I have another suggestion. We should have someone to show our guests around and answer their questions.
James:	Miss Wood is the best candidate, I think. She can speak both Mandarin and Cantonese fluently.
Dongbao:	Ms. Yang can do the job, too. It's necessary to have two people ready for the job.
Henry:	Good. I'll think it over later. I've one more thing to discuss with both of you. We need to draft an opening speech.
James:	Michelle wrote the speech last year. We can ask her to do it.
Dongbao:	No, she is on holiday now.
Henry:	Then, we have to do it ourselves now. Let me check my diary to see when I'll have time. Well, we can discuss the opening speech this Thursday 4 p.m. in my office. Can you both come to my office?
Dongbao & James:	All right. We'll be there at four o'clock Thursday afternoon.

Dialogue D   Pet

Walking out of a shopping center on Huaihai Road, Ying stops in front of a pet shop.

Ying:	Richard, come here and have a look. They are so cute, aren't they?
Richard:	Yes they are. Do you like rabbits?
Ying:	Of course. Look at those white fluffy fur and long ears. They are so adorable. When I was a kid, my mum told me that there is a very beautiful lady living on the moon with a very smart rabbit.
Richard:	Is that the story about Chang'e and the Jade Rabbit?
Ying:	Yes. The Jade Rabbit makes herbal medicine and is constantly pounding the elixir of life for the lady. Those elixirs grant her eternal life and keep her eternal youth.
Richard:	That's just one of many Asian bedtime stories, I think.
Ying:	Maybe. But in a clear night with full moon in the sky, you can see the shape of the rabbit.
Richard:	Now I know what you are thinking?
Ying:	Me?

Richard:	You want to have a little pet to make those pills for you, don't you?
Ying:	(*Culdn't help giggling.*)
Richard:	But rabbits are very smelly, you know, when they poop or pee. Especially when you have to keep them indoor all the time. What do you think of this?
Ying:	What? A Guinea Pig?
Richard:	Yep.
Ying:	No. They are just a bigger version of mouse. Despite their common name, these animals are not in the pig family, nor are they from Guinea. They are very active at night and make a lot of noises. Most important, they are not as cute as their Disney cousins.
Richard:	Mickey Mouse?
Ying:	Yep. Nothing beats Mickey Mouse.
Richard:	Not always. I do remember that you said you love the innocent eyes of the Puss in Boots in *Shrek*.
Ying:	Yes I do love big eyes.
Richard:	Check out this Chihuahua, it has super big eyes.
Ying:	Chihuahua is just too small. It even can't bark like a real dog.
Richard:	How about that Jack Russell puppy over there. Jack Russell is a typically small but very active and fearless type of dog. It is a unique terrier which has been preserved in working ability as well as appearance much as it existed over 200 years ago. It is principally white-bodied smooth, rough or broken-coated and origins in hunting fox.
Ying:	You know that I don't want a small dog.
Richard:	Then, it might be a good idea to have a look at the Labrador. They are supposed to be big.
Ying:	Really?
Richard:	The Labrador is the most popular breed of dog in the US. They are very loving, kind, loyal and compassionate to their master. It is being widely used by police and other official bodies for their detection and working abilities. Typically, Labradors are athletic and love to swim, play catch and retrieve games, are good with young children, and for protection.
Ying:	I saw those puppies on a TV ad about toilet papers. How big will they be when they become adult?
Richard:	Hard to say, though. The male ones can grow to about 60 center meters high and 30 to 60 kg. The female ones are little bit smaller in size and probably 5 to 20 kg less.
Ying:	Wow, they are huge. I think maybe it's just too big for me. Dogs with

that size could eat a lot everyday and it requires plenty excises to keep them healthy and happy. I travel too much and don't have a lot of time to look after them.

Richard: That's right. The responsibility and time dedicated to the loyal four-leg friends aren't something you just jump up and say I'll do it.

Ying: Then I'd better take your words as a friendly advice and stay away from pets.

Richard: Haha. You are getting smarter every day.

Notes

1. the volume, texture, speed and pitch	音量、音质、语速和音高
2. facial expression and body posture.	面部表情和身体姿态
3. a reward system	奖励制度,回报机制
4. cheer staff up	振奋员工的精神
5. a communication note	一份通报
6. last but not the least	最后但依然是很重要的一点
7. home renovation	住房装修
8. a tough job	一件艰苦的工作
9. lose heart	丧失勇气,失去信心
10. The lady's touch.	还是女士行啊!(对女性的恭维话,指其对事物的鉴赏力或洞察力很好。)
11. for the time being	暂时,目前
12. to redo the laundry	重新装修洗衣房
13. 5-tier shelf	五层的架子
14. You are the queen.	你说了算。
15. a solar hot water system	太阳能热水器
16. carbon footprint	碳足迹
17. bill	账单
18. plumber	管道工
19. demo (demonstration)	演示;示范
20. in charge of ...	主管
21. 8 stands	八个展台
22. function room	多功能厅
23. Couldn't agree more.	完全同意。
24. SME (small to medium-size enterprises)	中小型企业
25. settings	展厅的环境布置

26. official slogan	(公司)正式宣传口号
27. a symbolistic background	象征主义风格的背景图案
28. landmark architectures	标志性建筑
29. diarize	记录(在工作手册或日记中)
30. draft an opening speech	起草开幕演说词
31. Chang'e	嫦娥
32. Jade Rabbit	玉兔
33. elixir of life	仙丹
34. eternal youth	永远年轻
35. poop or pee	大小便
36. Guinea Pig	几内亚猪(常被用来做医学试验,也可作宠物)
37. Disney cousins	迪斯尼乐园的同类卡通动物(此处指米老鼠)
38. Mickey Mouse	米老鼠
39. Puss in Boots in *Shrek*	(电影)《怪物史莱克》中的普斯猫
40. Chihuahua	吉娃娃(小型犬,也称作芝娃娃、奇娃娃等)
41. Jack Russell	杰克·拉瑟短腿狗
42. puppy	小狗
43. terrier	[动]㹴(狗的一种)
44. Labrador	拉布拉多猎犬(常用为警卫或导盲)

Functional Expressions

Asking for Advice

1. Could you give me some advice on how to make up for the time I've lost?
2. Do you think I should change my plan?
3. I would appreciate some advice about the mortgage.
4. I would esteem your advice on our decision.
5. I'd like to have your advice about my research.
6. What should I do to solve this problem?
7. What do you think I should do?
8. What would you do if you were in my shoes?
9. What would you do in my position?
10. Would you recommend me to accept his invitation?

Advising Somebody to Do Something

1. Don't you think it might be a good idea to stay inside?

2. I think you might enjoy a holiday on the beach.
3. I'd never goof around, if I were you.
4. I'd stay over there, if I were in your shoes.
5. In my opinion, you should go on a diet.
6. It'll do you good to have a rest.
7. My suggestion would be to draw up a list of guests for the dinner.
8. Take my advice and leave it as it is.
9. Why don't you talk to her about it?
10. You'd better go through your test paper again.

Advising Somebody not to Do Something

1. Believe me and don't put any salt in it.
2. How about giving up sweets to lose weight?
3. I don't consider it's your business to handle this matter.
4. I don't think you should keep silent.
5. I wouldn't dip my bread into the soup, if I were you. It's not polite.
6. It's up to you but I wouldn't do that.
7. Take my advice and don't drive too fast.
8. The way I see it, you should avoid quarreling with her.
9. Why don't you finish typing this letter first?
10. You would be wise enough not to offend your boss.

Making Suggestions

1. Do you think it would be a good idea to name the baby Steve?
2. Have you ever thought of dining out this Friday evening?
3. How about giving him a free hand and see how it will turn out?
4. How about this idea: we have our summer vacation on the beach instead?
5. I know what we can do. Let's call a taxi.
6. I think it'd be a great idea to have a round of tennis.
7. I wonder whether you'd like to go to a jazz-club Saturday night.
8. I'll tell you what — why don't we move our headquarters to Moscow?
9. It might be a good idea to put it in a safe.
10. One idea would be to put up an ad in the newspaper.
11. Why don't we adopt a child?
12. Why don't you freshen up with a hot bath?
13. Would it be better to put up the shutter now?
14. You might as well see him now he is here.
15. You might like to xerox this article?

Making Negative Responses

1. I don't think I will, but thank you all the same.
2. I'd like that, but I can't afford the time.
3. I'm afraid your proposal is not acceptable.
4. It's an idea, I suppose, but it may cost a lot of money.
5. It's nice of you to ask, but I don't think so.
6. No, don't bother.

 ## Communicative Task

A Virtual Image

Types of Task: group, class.

Functions Practiced: describing a person's characteristics, making suggestions, asking for advice, advising someone to do something, advising someone not to do something.

Pre-task

1. Read the following list of Adjectives of Character and Physique individually. Use a dictionary if necessary. These are some typical adjectives we use to describe a person's character and physique. Keeping a list like this may help you a lot in your learning.

Adjectives of Character and Physique

active	bold	cunning	diabolical
eccentric	feeble	frank	generous
healthy	hysterical	ingenious	jealous
keen	loyal	manly	mean
muscular	nervous	opportunistic	proud
quarrelsome	righteous	shy	sickly
sportive	strong	tall	tough
ugly	violent	weak	willing
x-rated	youthful	vigorous	zealous

cunning	狡猾的,[美口](孩子等)伶俐的,可爱的,迷人的
diabolical	恶魔似的,穷凶极恶
eccentric	古怪的;偏执的
hysterical	歇斯底里的
ingenious	有创造性的和想象力的

x-rated   非常野蛮的，极其粗暴的

2. Select three adjectives in the list to make up three sentences. The subjects of the sentences can be some people in real life and known by your classmates (for example, some well known persons, movie actors or actresses), or some heroes (heroines) in novels, movies or dramas. The adjectives you select should fit the characters and/or physiques of the subjects in your sentences and later on must be accepted by your group members for the relevancy.

3. Read your sentences to your group members and seek their advice on your writing of the subjects in your sentences. Remember to use the sentences provided in Functional Expressions when you ask for advice.

4. Select ten best sentences in your group's writings, copy them both on your personal notebook and on a sheet of paper with a mark pen (white board marker), and post it on the wall.

5. When all of the groups have posted their works, read them one by one and exchange your opinions within your group members, focusing on language points (forms of language) and relevancy as well. Take notes when you find a vividly phrased sentence with an appropriately used adjective. Your notes will be used in the next step.

6. Now go back to your group and make **A New List of Adjectives of Character and Physique** like the one above in the English alphabetic order, for example, assertive, *brave*, *clever*, and so on. Your list must at least include twelve adjectives.

Task Procedure

1. In completing the task, select a group in your class as your twin group and decide which group is going to compose a descriptive passage for Miss Virtual and which one for Mister Virtual.

2. Miss Virtual and Mister Virtual are your imaginary creatures or the "virtual images". Their Characters and Physiques are in your hands and the power of the Adjectives you used in your description.

3. To write a good and "internally consistent" passage for these two virtual images you have to treat them as human beings. Now work in your group and together fill out the following table.

Instructions: a. Put an X in the square to indicate which one your group is going to
             write.

          b. Decide age, education, profession and hobby. You are welcome to add
             more information.

          c. Select adjectives from your notes and write down in blank space under
             Character and Physique.

Features of Character and Physique

☐ Miss Virtual
☐ Mister Virtual

Age	Proper Adjectives	
	Character	Physique
	1.	1.
Education	2	2
	3.	3.
Profession	4.	4.
	5.	5.
Hobby	6.	6.
	7.	7.
	8.	8.
	9.	9.
	10.	10.

4. Suggestions and advice, positive or negative, should be used when you and your group members are discussing the choice of adjectives. You are also allowed to come and go for the posted lists of adjectives on the wall.

5. Decide which one of your group members to do the passage writing. Others continue to search for appropriate adjectives and add them to your personal notebook while make offers to the writer.

6. During the process, you may check your notes from time to time to make suggestions or offer advice to the group and the writer.

7. When finished read the passage in your group. Make revisions if necessary.

8. Exchange your final version with your twin group.

9. Read the passage from your twin group to everyone in your group.

10. Mark your twin group's passage.

11. The pass standard is at least 10 adjectives used for the description of **Character and Physique.** The standard of Excellence is 14 adjectives properly used.

12. If 14 adjectives are appropriately used in your twin group's passage, give them a score of 80. If 10 used, mark the passage with the score of 60. Scores between 60 and 80 apply to any number of adjectives used between 10 and 14.

13. If more than 14 are well used in your twin group's passage, submit it to your teacher and make a suggestion to read it to your class.

Unit Seven

Agreement and Disagreement

 **Warm Up**

1. Say out Loud and Fast

1) It's only a small disagreement. Let's not make an issue of it.

2) I am in total disagreement with you as to the true of his words.

3) With an eye to future business, we agree to give you 12% discount.

4) After all, the committee will have the final say on the safe use of pesticides.

5) Shall I say we have reached an identical opinion on the issue of the next delivery date?

6) Richard urged to set aside differences because the challenges were great.

7) China and the United States have kept different statistics and disagreement with regard to the issue of bilateral trade volume.

8) There are a variety of ways that these issues can be addressed in a unanimous shareholders agreement.

9) Let's seek common ground while putting aside differences on the relocation of our Hangzhou office.

10) The global disparity in access to broadband around the world and the cost of a connection is revealed by UN figures.

2. Culture Tip

People may have different viewpoints on the same thing, partly because they have been brought up with different cultures and subcultures and partly because they are in different social positions. So it is very important for you to keep it in your mind that there are different ways to express yourself for different occasions and agree or disagree with others' ideas and opinions in a proper way.

Occasions can be roughly divided into two categories: formal and informal. A formal occasion would be in a shop, a business meeting, an interview, a political meeting, a government or state occasion, or among upper class people. An informal occasion would be a party, a casual visit, meeting someone on the street, a chat between friends, workmates and schoolmates, or among lower class people, etc. But then there can be some overlap. There are few hard and fast rules in English speaking communities and it really takes experience to know what phrases to use, when and how to use them.

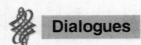 **Dialogues**

Dialogue A   A Plan for Spring Festival

In their bedroom, Henry and his wife Sophia are discussing their plan for the Spring Festival.

Henry: Sophia, I've just realized the Spring Festival is coming. Where should we spend our holiday?

Sophia: We can go to Harbin if you want. I remember you said you want to go there last time.

Henry: No, I don't think so.

Sophia: Why not?

Henry: Because Isabel will be with us this time. We shouldn't leave her alone at home. Also, Richard and his girlfriend want to discuss their plan for their engagement party with us. Their engagement party will also be around the Spring Festival, I am sure.

Sophia: I couldn't agree more. Spring Festival is the most important holiday to all Chinese people. We can go to Harbin next winter.

Henry: I absolutely agree.

Sophia: Then what particular ideas do you have?

Henry: This Spring Festival we will stay at home. We'll take Isabel to do some shopping along Nanjing Road and show her the Bund, the Pearl Tower. She hasn't been there before.

Sophia: That's good. What about Richard's engagement party?

Henry: We'll invite Ying and her parents to our home next week and discuss the details of the plan for the engagement.

Sophia: Shall we have dinner with them at home after the discussing?

Henry: I plan to eat out. We can book a table in a decent restaurant. The next day, we can have a party at home and invite our friends to come over.

Sophia: Why not ask our friends to go out with us instead? We can introduce Ying's parents to them.

Henry: No, not a good idea. The discussion of the engagement is supposed to be private.

Sophia: Yep, you're right.

Henry: We'll have the party the day after at home for our friends.

Sophia: OK. That would be more considerate. Henry, now we need to work out the guest list for the engagement party.

Henry: Is it too early to work out the list?

Sophia: No. If we want to make this engagement party a big one with forty or fifty guests to attend, we must get everything ready several months before the Spring Festival.

Henry: Why?

Sophia: Restaurant reservation for weddings in Shanghai usually should be made half a year before, even a year before. That's what I heard about at the office.

Henry: I see what you mean, but engagement is different from wedding and we can . . .

Sophia: Henry, the points are the number of the guests and the location of the restaurant. I want to make sure we hold the engagement banquet at a magnificent restaurant.

Henry: I've got exactly the same idea. OK, let's start to draw up the list of the guests we want to invite.

Dialogue B   Changes in Pudong

At the Pudong International Airport, Richard is sitting in a coffee bar and chatting with an old gentleman, Mr. Zhiming Zhang, while waiting for his girlfriend to arrive.

Mr. Zhang: What do you think of the new airport?

Richard: In my view, it's one of the most beautiful airports in the world.

Mr. Zhang: I'm of entirely the same opinion. I agree with you. Shanghai is changing very fast every day.

Richard: That's exactly what I want to say. I've been in Shanghai for almost five years and have seen the great changes day by day.

Mr. Zhang: I'm sixty-two and living in Pudong for most of my life. Before 1978 it was all farm land and there were few factories, few modern houses and only narrow paths here and there. I had lived in a small hut with a family of seven until I got married. If I wanted to buy things I had to walk a long distance, because there was no shop nearby.

Richard: But things are different now, aren't they?

Mr. Zhang: Yes. Since 1978, especially since 1992, Pudong has changed a lot. The government policy encourages the development of local economy. Do you agree with me?

Richard: Yes, that's just what I was thinking. A good policy can promote the economy smoothly and rapidly. What's the change of your family life?

Mr. Zhang: I've moved into a new apartment. My parents have their own apartment and my wife and I have our own apartment as well. Our children live near our new apartment.

Richard: Do you still need to go a long distance to buy things now?

Mr. Zhang: No, not any more. There are several supermarkets and chain stores near our apartment. Two of them are open 24 hours a day. It is much more convenient to buy things than before.

Richard: Well, good for you.

Mr. Zhang: The largest supermarket in Shanghai is also located in Pudong. And now we have this new airport. I believe Pudong will be more prosperous in future.

Richard: I believe that too. But are you here to meet someone?

Mr. Zhang: No. I enjoy sitting here, watching people passing by. I'm retired, you know. Are you meeting your friends or ...

Richard: My girlfriend. Well, her flight will be landing in a few minutes. I'm going to the arrival gate.

Mr. Zhang: Good to talk to you, young man, and hope to see you again some day.

Dialogue C   On the Way Home

Richard and his girlfriend are in a taxi on their way home from the airport.

Ying: Did you miss me?

Richard: Of course. I kept seeing you in my dreams.

Ying: So did I.

Richard: What do you think of France?

Ying: I must say France is a very beautiful and friendly country. There're many famous and grand theaters in Paris, too.

Richard: You visited many friends there, didn't you? Did they come to watch you dance?

Ying:	Yes. I also went to see your friends in my free time.
Richard:	Good. I haven't seen them for ages. Are they all right there?
Ying:	They're all very well.
Richard:	What did they say?
Ying:	They said they were eager to visit China.
Richard:	I'll invite them to visit Shanghai sometime next year. Did you write all their addresses down for me?
Ying:	Yes. Here is the address book they gave to me at the airport.
Richard:	That's good. Thank you.
Ying:	How are your parents?
Richard:	They're quite well. They're waiting for you at home and we'll have dinner together.
Ying:	I've bought some presents for them.
Richard:	What are they?
Ying:	A pair of watches for them. (*Ying takes out those watches from her hand bag and shows them to Richard.*) Do you think they are nice?
Richard:	Boy, oh, boy! How beautiful they are! I think they'll like these beautiful and precious gifts. Any presents for me?
Ying:	Of course! (*Ying is giggling.*)
Richard:	Do you want to tell me what it is?
Ying:	No. It's a secret. Look, we are almost home. I'll show you later.
Richard:	OK. (*Richard then talks to the taxi driver.*) Excuse me, could you please pull over there, in front of the yellow building?
Ying:	Don't forget the large bag in the trunk, Richard.
Richard:	OK. I know.

Dialogue D   New Products

A lot of guests are coming to the show hosted by Shanghai Computer Company. Ms. Linda Yang is showing them the new Desktop ZF Series and answering their questions.

Guest A:	Excuse me. May I ask some questions about this new computer?
Linda:	Of course. You're welcome to ask anything about our products.
Guest A:	I'd like to get a general idea about this computer and what it can do.
Linda:	All right. This is our new Desktop ZF Series. It has a unique all-in-one design to handle the needs of medium-to-large organizations. Packed with professional-grade components and energy-efficient features. It is the new generation of business computer.

Guest A: What does all-in-one mean?

Linda: It means all the main components, like the processor, the memory, the blu-ray drive and the hard drive, are packed at the back of the display screen. It not only saves space, with only 1.2 inches in thickness, but also eliminates the maintenance hassles. For example, all components are replaceable and upgradeable which means you can upgrade the whole computer to a totally different one in less than 5 minutes.

Guest A: Very impressive.

Linda: Thank you. The ZF Series use modules made with post-consumer recycled content to help minimize environmental impact and meet ENERGY STAR 4.0 requirements. Our special designed Power Manager software can help you save energy up to 80%. With newly designed optional Solar-Power Pack you can power the ZF Series from renewable energy source.

Guest B: (*Pointing to the small metal bar on the bottom of the screen.*) Excuse me, what is this thing?

Linda: This is a fingerprint reader. Swipe your finger over it, it will read your fingerprint and login you to the system. Just like the one you've seen on the movies.

Guest B: Ha-ha. Like those FBI agents do.

Linda: Yes. Besides that, you can combine it with our latest face detection system to stop unauthorized user access. The face detection system uses the built-in HD webcam to detect movements and to analyze faces against the data stored in centre database. We believe that system security and data safety are two most important aspects for business users.

Guest C: What is the specification of this one?

Linda: It powers with an Intel 64-bit quad-core CPU at 4.78GHz, 8GB memory, 64GB SSD and 1TB hard drive. The SSD drive is for operating system only to ensure the best performance. The best part is this multi-touch screen. You can use it as a mouse replacement, zooming, rotating and drawing. It responds to multiple touches at the same time.

Guest D: What about connectivity?

Linda: It has six USB 3.0 ports, two on the left side and four on the right side. It also has two eSATA/USB combined ports which support sleep and charge. Wireless g/n network, Bluetooth, gigabyte network port, HDMI port. Two external monitor ports allow you to connect with two screens up to 23 inches to triple your display area.

Guest A: What's the price range?

Linda: It depends on what modules and features you want. The basic model starts from 9,000RMB. The high-end model with all features could be around 24,000RMB. If you are more interested in this ZF Series, I can introduce you to our General Manage Mr. Henry White.

Guest A： Thanks. I want to have a look at other computers first before I talk to him.

Linda： No worries. Let me know when you want to talk to him.

Guest A： OK. I will.

Ms. Yang： Thank you very much. The next section is mobile and portable computer section. Mr. Wood will show you our latest laptops, netbooks, and touch pads.

Notes

1.	hard and fast rules	不可改变的规则
2.	engagement party	订婚派对
3.	book a table	预定餐桌
4.	I'm of entirely the same opinion.	我的看法完全一样。
5.	the opening and reform policy	改革开放政策
6.	giggling	偷笑
7.	pull over	把(车)靠在路边
8.	Desktop ZF Series	ZF 系列桌上型电脑
9.	all-in-one	一体机
10.	blu-ray drive	蓝光光盘驱动
11.	maintenance hassles	维修的烦恼
12.	display screen	显示屏
13.	post-consumer recycled content	消费者使用后的日常生活废弃物
14.	ENERGY STAR 4.0 requirements	美国环境保护署的能源之星 4.0 标准
15.	Power Manager software	电源管理程序
16.	optional Solar-Power Pack	可选太阳能电源
17.	fingerprint reader	指纹阅读器
18.	FBI agent	美国联邦调查局特工
19.	face detection system	脸部识别系统
20.	to stop unauthorized user access	阻止非授权人员使用计算机
21.	HD webcam	高清晰度网络照相机
22.	SSD（solid-state drive）	固体磁盘
23.	Intel 64-bit quad-core CPU	美国英特尔公司生产 64 位四核芯片
24.	Hz（Hertz）	赫兹(计算频率的单位)
25.	multi-touch screen	多点触摸屏
26.	zooming, rotating and drawing	放大缩小,旋转与绘画

27. eSATA（external Serial Advanced Technology　外置串行高级控制器
    Attachment)
28. sleep and charge　　　　　　　　　　　计算机睡眠与充电姿态
29. bluetooth　　　　　　　　　　　　　　蓝牙
30. gigabyte network port　　　　　　　　千兆网络接口
31. HDMI（High-Definition Multimedia Interface)高清多媒体接口
32. the mobile and portable computer section　移动与便携电脑展示区
33. laptop　　　　　　　　　　　　　　　笔记本电脑
34. netbook　　　　　　　　　　　　　　上网本
35. touch pad　　　　　　　　　　　　　平板触摸电脑

 ## Functional Expressions

Asking If Somebody Agrees

1. All right with you?
2. Do you agree with me?
3. Don't you agree?
4. Don't you think she's a bright student?
5. Don't you think so?
6. He's quite old, isn't he?
7. I wonder if you would agree that money doesn't mean happiness.
8. Money is losing its value, wouldn't you say?
9. OK with you?
10. OK?
11. Right?
12. Would you agree with what I said just now?
13. Wouldn't you say so?

Agreeing

1. Dead right.
2. Exactly.
3. How right that is!
4. How true you are!
5. I absolutely agree.
6. I couldn't agree more.
7. I suppose so.

8. I think I'm with you there.

9. I'm confident I'd go along with you there.

10. I'm sure you're right.

11. I've got exactly the same idea.

12. That's just my own opinion.

13. That's just what I was thinking.

14. That's right.

15. True enough.

16. Well, that's the thing.

17. You know that's exactly what I think.

Partly Agreeing

1. Could be, but he's not experienced.

2. I agree with much of what you said, but things are not so easy.

3. I can see that, but it may cause trouble.

4. I couldn't agree more, but there may be a sudden rain tomorrow.

5. I see what you mean, but we must take everything into account.

6. I see your point, but pollution is still a problem.

7. I take your point, but a reporter never goes deeply into any one subject.

8. In spite of what you say, I think perhaps we'd better be careful about it.

9. May be, but don't you think it's too late?

10. That may be true, but industry's making us wealthier.

11. There's a lot in what you say, but we don't have enough money.

12. To a certain extent, yes, but it's hard to put it into practice.

13. Well, you have a point there, but a lot of people have fun playing football.

14. Yes, but don't you think it's too noisy?

15. Right, but we shouldn't forget the road condition.

16. Sure, but, perhaps, there're other problems.

Disagreeing

1. Are you kidding?

2. But isn't it more a matter of population?

3. But isn't it more to do with the cost of living?

4. I couldn't agree with you less.

5. I don't think so.

6. I don't think you're right there.

7. I wouldn't say that.

8. I'm afraid I have a different opinion.

9. I'm not at all convinced by your explanation.

10. Not at all!

11. Not really.

12. Personally, I'd be more inclined to agree with Terry Robert.

13. That's not how I see it.

14. That's not the way I see it.

15. You can't mean that!

16. That's your opinion, not mine.

Admitting You Are Wrong and Somebody Else Is Right

1. OK, you win.

2. Sorry, I got it all wrong.

3. Yes, I have to admit you are right.

4. Give me a minute, perhaps I'm wrong there.

5. I think perhaps you have a point there.

Coming to an Agreement

1. Everyone's happy about the decision, then.

2. Good, that's agreed then.

3. Looks like we've agreed where to go.

4. So what are we arguing about?

5. That's it, then.

6. We are agreed on that.

7. Well, that's settled then.

 ## Communicative Task

Life and Life Skills

Types of Task: pair, group, class.

Functions Practiced: agreeing, disagreeing, asking if somebody agrees, coming to an
agreement.

Pre-task

1. Read the table below. This table shows some important things in different stages of
life. People have quite opposite views on life. Some say, "Life is a cup of bitter wine" as
sung in many pop songs. Others argue, "Life is fun, sweet and beautiful" as shown in many

films.

2. Examine and tick off some items under the column **Things** in the table that you think are important in relation to different stages of a person's life.

Things \ Stages	Under 10	11~20	21~40	41~60	61+
Ambition					
Family					
Food					
Friendship					
Health					
Job					
Love					
Money					
Confidence					
Self-esteem					

3. What stage of life are you in? What are the top five important things you have selected for that stage? Why?

4. Take out a piece of paper and write down these top five important things at the stage of your life now and their reasons.

5. Write a short paragraph about 200 words on the topic "The meaning of life as I see it".

Task Procedure

1. Work with your pair to compare and discuss the most important things at different stages of life as suggested in your completed table.

2. Exchange your ideas on the topic "The meaning of life as I see it" with your pair and prepare a new paragraph by combining all your ideas in it and rename the paragraph "The meaning of life as we see it".

3. When you complete the task, raise your hand to let your teacher know.

4. Your teacher will select two voluntary pairs to read their essays before your class.

5. Listen and try to jot down on your notepad the main points from the speakers.

6. Go back to your regular group and together read the introductory part of the life skills below.

Introduction to Life Skills

Whether you are at elementary, secondary or tertiary school, some life skills are important to all individuals. Life skills differ from regular school rules because they apply to all groups in all situations. They form the basis for agreement between teachers and students, and among the students about behaviors and expectations (social and academic), as both of you perceive their importance in school and society.

7. Read the following table and add to the list if you think some other skills are also important to achieve one's personal best in life.

Life Skills	Definition	Order of Importance	
		Academic	Social
Caring			
Common Sense	to use good judgment		
Cooperation	to work together toward common goal or purpose		
Courage	to act according to one's belief		
Curiosity			
Creativity			
Effort	to do your best		
Empathy	to identify with and understand other's feelings, and motives		
Flexibility	to be willing to alter plans when necessary		
Friendship			
Initiative	to do something of one's own free will, because it needs to be done		
Integrity	to act according to a sense of what's right and wrong		
Organization	to plan, arrange, and implement in an orderly way		
Patience	to wait calmly for someone or something		
Perseverance	to keep at it		
Pride	satisfaction from doing your personal best		
Problem Solving	to create solutions in difficult situations and everyday problems		
Responsibility			
Sense of Humor	to laugh and be playful without harming others		

8. Some of the definitions are given in the table above. For those undefined skills, discuss with your group members first and then write down your own definitions in the table.

9. Compare your definitions with the others' in your group and discuss with each other until you all come to an agreement.

10. Individually, take a minute to put them in order of importance by yourself.

11. Use the Functional expressions learned in this unit to offer your agreements or disagreements in your discussion after all of your group members have reordered the list against the criteria of your personal choice.

12. The next step is to tick off three skills you think are most important in order to be successful in academic learning in school, three skills you think you possess and are well practiced, and three other skills you think you are not good at.

13. Show your list to your group and ask them if they agree or disagree with your self-evaluation.

14. Discuss in your group who is the person in your class possessing the most life skills in the above table. When you discover the right person, you should justify yourself and explain with supporting examples to your group members.

15. Report your discovery to your class.

16. You may offer your agreement or disagreement at the end of each reporting.

Unit Eight

Like and Dislike

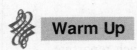 **Warm Up**

1. Say out Loud and Fast

1) My mother dislikes seeing you with me.

2) She finds him most objectionable.

3) He was repulsed by what he saw.

4) Almost every one dislikes getting up early in our dorm.

5) I would become disgusted with my futile daydreams.

6) It is to the students' credit that they hate war and social injustice.

7) I hate to mention it, but you still owe me five pounds from last week.

8) He is fond of the atmosphere of peace and calm in the country.

9) I suppose I shall have to include my insufferable relatives in the wedding party.

10) I like the way I like, you like the way you like. Both of us dislike the way we dislike.

2. Culture Tip

Saying what your like or dislike can be quite difficult, especially when someone is asking for your opinion on something they want to buy or have already bought. The skill of being tactful is one that takes experience of a culture firsthand and of the people involved.

Being tactful involves knowing suitable phrase and tone of voice. Pitch, intonation, volume and texture are crucial when you want to express your likes and dislikes in a tactful way.

One general piece of advice for you is to sound natural when speaking English and not as robotic as is the habit of many second language speakers. When you are listening to native

English speakers, listen to their pitch, intonation, volume and texture. But also keep in mind the situation they are speaking in — it will effect how they talk.

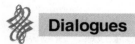 **Dialogues**

Dialogue A   Music

Richard has invited some of his friends to his home. They are chatting and listening to music in the sitting room.

Richard:	Luke, what kind of music do you like?
Luke:	Pop music. I'm crazy about it. And you?
Richard:	I'm keen on pop music as well, but I also like classical music.
Mary:	I really don't like pop music.
Anne:	Neither do I. I can't stand the monotonous rhythm and unoriginal tunes.
Ying:	I prefer Chinese folk songs. They're very melodious.
Richard:	After I knew Ying, I began to have a fancy for Chinese songs. They are wonderful. And I also get extra benefits from listening to Chinese songs. You see, I am learning Chinese while enjoying the music.
Mary:	Me too. It's a good way to learn to speak Chinese by listening to Chinese songs. Some of my friends studying in Fudan University are mad about Chinese music. They have even organized a Chinese music club.
Anne:	What do they do in this music club?
Mary:	They've invited a famous musician as their teacher and rehearse several programs twice a month. They love to sing Chinese songs and they speak Chinese fluently.
Richard:	Do they often give performance at Fudan University?
Mary:	Yes. They're often invited to perform not only at Fudan, but also other universities and colleges. They're welcomed everywhere.
Luke:	I'll be very glad if I have a chance to watch their performance.
Mary:	You can go to Fudan University this Saturday evening. They'll be performing in the Students' Club.
Luke:	OK. I'll go there. Who else would like to go with me?
Richard:	Luke, I'd like to go with you. How about you, Ying?
Ying:	I wish I could go with you. But I'm busy this Saturday evening. Thank you for asking, Richard.
Anne:	I'll be there.

Luke: Do you want me to pick you up, Anne?

Anne: No, thanks. I can take a bus.

Dialogue B   A New Look

After months of renovation Mr. White's home takes on a new look now. Sophia is showing her friends around.

Helen: Hi, Sophia. How are you?

Sophia: I'm good. Thank you.

Nancy: Hi, Sophia. Nice to see you again.

Sophia: Nice to see you too. Come in and take a seat.

Nancy: (*After seated.*) So this is it?

Sophia: Yep, after months of hard work and lots of money. Finally, this place gets a new look.

Helen: It's really nice. I like the color of the walls.

Sophia: Thank you, it's my choice. The workers just couldn't get the color right. We had to repaint the walls three times.

Nancy: Things are harder to do here, especially when you can't speak Chinese.

Sophia: That's right. Maybe it's the time for me to learn some Chinese. Now, let me show you around.

(*Stand up and walk to the sitting room.*)

Helen: Look at those sofas. The leather is so soft and smooth.

Sophia: These are Henry's favorite. He's kind of obsessed with leather seats. All his chairs at home and in the office are all leather ones. He loves the feeling of touching those natural materials, and the comfort and relaxation that gives him when seating on it.

Nancy: I'm crazy about leather too. But only for purse and shoes.

Helen: That's true. All women like purse and shoes. I am no exception. Ha-ha.

Sophia: Those single seats are recliners. When you sit on it, and pull the lever on the side, the back of the chair will tilt backwards and the legrest will automatically move up to support the legs. Now, Nancy, sit down in the recliner and have a try.

Nancy: Yes, the back is lowering. Gee, the legrest is rising, too.

Sophia: Do you like it, Nancy?

Nancy: Very much indeed. I like its style, too.

Sophia: Now I'd like to show you the new furniture in our dinning room.

Helen: This new set of dinning table is very pretty, isn't it, Nancy?

Nancy:	Of course, it's nice.
Sophia:	It's Italian style. It was on sale. The whole set cost me only five thousand two hundred *yuan*. Henry and I like it very much.
Helen:	Where did you get it?
Sophia:	We bought it from the Friendship Store. Henry likes to buy things there. He says the ambience of the Friendship Store seems to encourage him to buy.
Nancy:	He's right. I enjoy shopping there, too. Sometimes I go to the Friendship Store for the pure fun of it.
Helen:	I do that too. I like window-shopping.
Sophia:	Come on. Let's go and see our redecorated kitchen.
Nancy:	Hey! You've got a new dishwasher.
Sophia:	And a new fridge, too. I have both built in the counter. The old ones always have something wrong and use too much electricity.
Helen:	Look at the layout. How nice! Sophia, you are really an excellent interior designer. Sophia, what's the maker of the fridge?
Sophia:	Haier. A famous company in China. They make quality home appliances. This is a new model with 5 star energy rating. Now let me make some coffee with our new coffee machine.

Dialogue C   In a Cafe

Richard and his girlfriend Ying are sitting in a cafe.

Waitress:	What can I do for you?
Richard:	One Cappuccino no sugar.
Ying:	I would like a glass of lemon juice, please.
Waitress:	Here you are. One lemon juice and one Cappuccino. Anything else?
Richard:	No, nothing for the moment, thank you.
Ying:	How're you doing these days, Richard?
Richard:	Just working, working on a new advertisement. Do you know anything about advertising?
Ying:	Not really. Of course, I've seen a lot of ads on TV, in magazine, and so on, but I don't think that's what you mean.
Richard:	No. Almost all our clients are industrial-based. We rarely put our clients' ads in the mass media unless they specifically ask us to do so.
Ying:	I suppose you put those adverts in trade journals?
Richard:	Yep. You're pretty smart. We advertise them in most of the major trade

journals, and in some of the professional magazines, too.

Ying: But in a way you still need to rely on some kind of media.

Richard: Of course. But we do publish our own brochure to introduce our clients' products.

Ying: Do you employ any artists?

Richard: We have one. She's known as a "visualizer". We also have a copywriter. He takes photographs we need as well. We're kept busy every day.

Ying: So what's your new job now?

Richard: I was a photographer in our company. I told you about that, right? But now my major work is to contact our clients cross all lines of business.

Ying: Do you like your new job?

Richard: Yeah, I enjoy the sense of achievement when our clients are satisfied with my service.

Ying: Richard, I want you to know I'm very proud of you.

Richard: This is what I like to hear from you. Well, the movie begins at 8:20. We'd better get going.

Ying: Would you wait for a while? I need to powder my nose.

Richard: OK. No problem.

Dialogue D   At a Flower Market

Mr. White and his wife are in a flower market. There are all kinds of beautiful flowers there.

Sophia: Oh, look, how nice these flowers are!

Henry: They're transported from the southern cities of China such as Kunming, Guangzhou, and so on.

Sophia: You seem to know a lot about the flower trade. But they could be from abroad.

Henry: Yep. Some of these flowers could be sent over to Shanghai from other countries by air. Look at these tulips. Aren't they lovely? They must have been imported from Holland.

Sophia: And they are expensive, I guess.

Henry: They are. 10 *yuan* each. Shall we buy some?

Sophia: How about five? Five will be good enough for our sitting room.

Henry: What else would you like to buy?

Sophia: I'd like to get some roses.

Henry: I prefer the chrysanthemums to the roses. They last longer.

Sophia: Roses are the symbol of happy life and love.

Henry: Chrysanthemums are the sign of happy holidays and solidarity.

Sophia: Then get both of them.

Henry: And the tulips.

（*Mr . and Mrs . White step into a flower shop .*）

Salesman: Good morning. What can I do for you?

Henry: I want to buy some roses，chrysanthemums and tulips.

Salesman: How many do you want?

Henry: Ten roses，ten chrysanthemums and five tulips.

Salesman: Red or yellow for the roses?

Sophia: Red，please. And how about the chrysanthemums，Henry?

Henry: Dark pink，and yellow tulips.

Sophia: I like these yellow tulips，too. They look fresh and pretty.

Salesman: You have keen eyes. The yellow tulips just arrived this morning. They came from Holland. But why don't you buy ten for each flower? I can give you a good deal. Nine for each tulip. Is that OK with you，ma'am?

Sophia: Sounds good. I take ten tulips.

Henry: How much are they?

Salesman: Ten *yuan* for the roses，seven for the chrysanthemum and ninety for the tulips. That makes one hundred and seven *yuan* in all.

Sophia: Here's two hundred *yuan* .

Salesman: Thank you. And here's the change，ninety-three *yuan* ，and your flowers. Thanks for coming. See you.

Notes

1.	the skill of being tactful	大方得体的（说话）技巧
2.	that takes experience of a culture firsthand	需要有对一种文化的第一手经验
3.	pop music	流行乐曲，通俗音乐
4.	be crazy about	热衷于……
5.	be keen on	对……有兴趣；喜爱……的
6.	classical music	古典音乐
7.	can't stand the monotonous rhythm	不能忍受单调的节奏
8.	unoriginal tunes	雷同的曲调
9.	Chinese folk songs	中国民歌
10.	very melodious	非常悦耳动听
11.	have a fancy for	特别偏爱……

12. extra benefits	额外的好处
13. rehearse several programs	排练多个节目
14. obsess with ...	对……着迷
15. recliner	躺椅
16. pull the lever	拉起手柄
17. legrest	搁脚板，脚托
18. Haier	海尔(家电企业名)
19. on sale	减价出售
20. the ambience of the Friendship Store	友谊商店的氛围
21. for the pure fun of it	仅仅为了消遣而已
22. window-shopping	只看不买,逛商店
23. redecorated kitchen	重新装修过的厨房
24. built in the counter	内置在橱柜里
25. use too much electricity	太费电
26. 5 star energy rating	五星节能级别
27. the maker of the fridge	冰箱的牌子
28. Cappuccino	卡布基诺咖啡
29. mass media	大众传播媒介
30. trade journal	行业杂志
31. She's known as a "visualizer".	她是"形象设计师"。
32. a copywriter	广告文编写人
33. sense of achievement	成就感
34. powder my nose	(女性)去卫生间
35. tulip	郁金香
36. chrysanthemums	菊花
37. I can give you a good deal.	我可以给你们一个好价钱。

 ## Functional Expressions

Asking If Somebody Likes Something or Somebody Else

1. Are you keen on disco?
2. Do you care for this color?
3. Do you enjoy having a summer holiday on the beach?
4. Do you go for jazz?
5. Do you like lots of free time?
6. Does Ernest fancy that girl?

7. Don't you like meeting people?
8. Don't you love that pavilion?
9. Isn't that scenery great?

Stating You Like Something or Somebody

1. Collecting stamps is a lovely way to pass the time.
2. I adore sailing.
3. I do like it when you accompany me.
4. I don't think I've seen anything I like better.
5. I have a fancy for that color.
6. I love that design.
7. I really care for that dog.
8. I really enjoy Shakespeare's *A Midsummer Night's Dream*.
9. I really go for oyster.
10. I'm crazy about skating.
11. I'm head over heals about the dress.
12. I'm mad about that man.
13. I'm nuts about diving.
14. I'm really sold on these dishes.
15. I'm very keen on outdoor sports.
16. I've always liked fishing.
17. There's nothing I enjoy more than attending a party.
18. Water-skiing is very enjoyable.
19. What I most enjoy is painting.
20. You can't beat hang-gliding.
21. Your story is really great.

Stating You Dislike Something or Somebody

1. Horrible, isn't it?
2. I can't bear for my daughter to go round with those rough boys.
3. I can't stand his rudeness.
4. I can't waken up any enthusiasm for that movie.
5. I couldn't like it less, I'm afraid.
6. I don't think I've ever seen anything I dislike more.
7. I find it difficult to get on with your brother.
8. I never could put up with my mom's inquisition.
9. I really hate gossiping.
10. I'm afraid I don't like that fellow.

11. I'm not very keen on traveling by air.

12. I've never liked fish, I'm afraid.

13. That sort of music is rubbish.

14. There's nothing I like less than lying.

15. There's nothing I like less.

Communicative Task

I Like/Dislike Students Who . . .

Types of Task: pair, group, class.

Functions Practiced: stating you like/dislike something or somebody, asking for personal
　　　　　　　　　　information, recalling a white lie in the past.

Pre-task

1. Work on your own to read the personal survey about Like/Dislike in your daily life.
Read the questions and fill out the "Why" part in the grid.

A Personal Survey

Do you Like or Dislike?	Why
Food: pizza, macaroni, spaghetti, sushi	
Drinks: mineral water, alcohols, milk, strong tea, beer	
Music: Rap, Techno, Disco, Country	
Sports: table tennis, soccer, volleyball, swiming, walking	
Places: small town, metropolis, tropical rainforest, prairie	
TV: sitcom, talk show, series	
Browsers: IE, Firefox, Chrome, Safari, Opera, 360	
Computer: desktop, laptop, touch pad, netbook	

2. Ask your pair the questions listed in the grid randomly with your pair's textbook
closed.

3. Ask some extra questions that occur to you as you go through the process of
questioning.

4. Roles are reversed after you've finished all the questions.

Task Procedure

1. Here are a few students you may have seen somewhere around you. You can add some more to the list by looking around in your class.

I Like/Dislike Students Who	
. . . in classroom	. . . outside classroom
make inappropriate noises	park their bikes at the dorm gate
give others appropriate compliments	keep shared materials organized
eat, drink, or sleep	eat crisps at the cinema
leave cellphone activated	jaywalk in the streets
wear inappropriate dress	walk gracefully
often talk disruptively	are kind to others
refuse to sit in assigned seat	are unprepared for class
chew gum	litter in public place
give others in appropriate compliments	jump queues in a check-out
raise hand to answer question	throw their used batteries into a field
give group members a fair share or turn	spit in the streets
damage the public property	speak vulgar language
help substitute teachers with equipments	jog every day
take an unexcused absence from class	behave like a well-educated person
act with responsibility	speak with a sense of humor
laugh at inappropriate times	dress fashionably

(Teacher may select some or all of behaviors and copy them on the blackboard for voting at the end of the task.)

2. Make a table on a piece of paper under the headings "I like students who . . ." on the left column, and "I dislike students who . . ." on the right column. See the sample below.

I like students who . . .	Reason	I dislike students who . . .	Reason

3. Under each column, list five kinds of students you either like or dislike.

4. Write down some phrases or expressions in the relevant grids under the column **Reason**.

5. In your group, ask each other why she/he likes and dislikes the particular group of students on the list. When you express your opinions, try to use the sentence patterns in this unit.

6. If you do not agree with each other on a certain kind of behavior, you may express your concern. For example, you might say, "I don't mind students who eat popcorn in the cinema. In fact I think they have the right to do so." Or you may say, "I don't like students who eat crisps in the cinema. Students who eat crisps in the cinema make a lot of noise and annoy me. They should eat them before the show."

7. If you cannot reach an agreement on certain kinds of student's behaviors, you may also turn to the other members in your group to seek more advice.

8. Look at the blackboard. Add all the behaviors and conducts that all of your classmates do not like to the list on the blackboard, if necessary.

9. Now comes the voting time. Select one student to read out the listed behaviors one by one and two other students to count the votes on "dislike" from the class.

10. Repeat the above step until all the items are voted, all the votes are counted and marked on the blackboard.

11. Copy down on your note the top five "dislikes" suggested by all your classmates. Use them as a warning guide to shape yourself in your daily life.

Unit Nine

Invitation

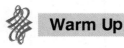 **Warm Up**

1. Say out Loud and Fast

1) On this special occasion of my birthday, I cordially invite you and your family to be present with me.

2) We look forward to seeing you on Sunday. For admittance, kindly bring the invitation with you.

3) If it is an invitation for Christmas, Valentine's Day or any significant occasion, you can also attach a themed prose along with your invitation letter.

4) Formal invitation letter format should contain the address of the inviter and the invitee as well.

5) We are cordially inviting Sophia White, General Manager of Oriental Travel Agency to visit our Headquarters of PanAm Tourism at Los Angels on Monday April 9 through April 17, 2012.

6) It's important to keep your dinner party invitation letter as simple, brief and focused as possible for fast and easy understanding.

7) The format and content of any invitation letter reflects the standard of the person inviting the people.

8) Invitation letter for informal occasions must be cordial, respectful and wholehearted.

9) Invitation letter for informal occasions should always make the invitee feel special and his presence in the occasion is most eagerly awaited.

10) To celebrate our success we are inviting all our valued customers and other delegates this Sunday to share the grand opening of our subsidiary Sunland Trading.

2. Culture Tip

The invitation may come from a community, international host family program, or from someone you have met in a social gathering. In making the invitation, the prospective host will telephone, speak to you in person, or send a written note. A written invitation includes the date, time, place, and a brief description of the occasion. If the written invitation bears the initials RSVP, it must be answered.

If you are invited to dinner at someone's home, it is wise to arrive between the hour stated and 10 minutes later. Many social affairs other than dinner give a range of time within which the invitees are expected to arrive. Receptions, seminars, cocktail parties, buffet suppers, picnics, etc. are such events.

Although it is always welcome, it is not necessary to bring flowers or a gift when you are invited to lunch or dinner, except on special occasions, such as a holiday. Should you wish to bring something, it should be small and simple. It is customary to bring the hostess a small present — often a book, a box of candy, a bottle of wine, or some similar gifts.

 **Dialogues**

Dialogue A   A Drink After Work

It's 5 o'clock Friday afternoon. Richard is still bound up with his work. David Smith, his colleague in the marketing department, comes up to him.

David: Do you have some time after work tonight?

Richard: Yeah. Why?

David: We're going out for a drink at Hard Stone's.

Richard: Good idea. Is there anything special to celebrate?

David: Why? No. Just to relax! You know we've been overworked for a week. Will you come?

Richard: I'd love to, but I'm afraid I can't. I have to finish this draft today.

David: Come on, boy. Don't work too hard.

Richard: The manager asked me to draft an ad of a new high-rise for a property development company. I haven't got any ideas, and the deadline is tomorrow.

David: Don't worry! It's good for you to go out and have fun. You know inspiration always sparkles at the most unexpected moment. Ideas may strike you when you reach the bar, after a drink or during the chatting with someone.

Richard:	It sounds quite reasonable. Maybe I really need a beer and some fresh air. OK. Let's go!
David:	Do you mind if we go Dutch, Richard?
Richard:	Of course not. By the way, who else is coming?
David:	Five more. Jane, Donna, Jiajia and Michelle. Mary is out at the moment, but she'll come back soon.
Richard:	I've never been to Hard Stone's. Is it far from here? How can we get there?
David:	You've got a car, haven't you?
Richard:	I see. That's why you talked me into it.
David:	You said it. In fact, we planed it yesterday, but I forgot to tell you. Sorry about that.
Richard:	Alright. I'll pick you up at the gate in half an hour.
David:	Good pal. See you.

Dialogue B   California Red '89

In his office Mr. White is calling Mr. William Brown to invite him and his wife, Mrs. Fanny Brown to a welcome dinner at his home.

William:	Hello, William speaking.
Henry:	Hello, William. It's me, Henry.
William:	Oh, Henry! How is everything going?
Henry:	Fine, thanks. I know your wife arrived in Shanghai yesterday. Sophia and I would like to invite you and your wife to have dinner at my house this Saturday.
William:	Thank you for inviting me and my wife. My wife will be happy to pay a visit to your home.
Henry:	At 7 p.m. Is it convenient for you?
William:	That's fine. At seven this Saturday evening. We'll be there then.
Henry:	Good. See you then.
William:	See you.
	(*At the Mr. White's.*)
Henry:	Welcome. Glad you could make it.
William:	Good evening. It is very kind of you to invite us. Henry, this is my wife, Fanny. Fanny, this is Mr. White.
Henry:	Nice to meet you, Mrs. Brown. This is my wife, Sophia.
Sophia:	How do you do, Mrs. Brown? I'm happy to meet you.
Fanny:	How do you do? Please call me Fanny.

William:	This is for you, Sophia. I hope you'll like it.
Sophia:	Thank you. May I open it?
William:	Sure.
Sophia:	Oh, it's a California Red, '89! That's very kind of you!
William:	I'm glad you like it.
Henry:	This is a vintage. Sophia, you know, a vintage wine is one made from grapes that were all, or primarily, grown and harvested in a single specified year. And it must be a good year to make the perfect taste.
Sophia:	Then it must be expensive, too.
Henry:	Of course, it is. We'll drink this vintage tonight. The general rule for wine is red meat or red sauces should be served with a red wine. White wine is the better choice when serving white meat such as fish and chicken. Sophia prepared roast beef and roasted pumpkin, which will match this vintage red wine perfectly.
Fanny:	It'll be a wonderful night for us.
Sophia:	Come into the living room, please. I'll show you our rooms.
Fanny:	Oh, what a lovely apartment you have here! Spacious living room, well furnished and gorgeous decoration.
Sophia:	Thank you. Please make yourself at home.

Dialogue C   RSVP

Mr. Dongbao Wang is on his way to work. He stops at the corner of a street and he decides to wait for Mr. White to show up.

Mr. Wang:	Morning, Mr. White.
Henry:	Morning, Mr. Wang.
Mr. Wang:	It's a fine day, isn't it?
Henry:	Yeah. The air is refreshing. It seems we'll have a sunny weekend.
Mr. Wang:	It's a good time to have an outdoor activity. Mr. William Brown is organizing a barbecue this Saturday. Are you coming?
Henry:	Yeah, I am. I got his invitation yesterday.
Mr. Wang:	I've got a question to ask you, Mr. White.
Henry:	I'm listening.
Mr. Wang:	On the invitation card, it says RSVP. What does it mean?
Henry:	This phrase comes from French, répondez s'il vous plaît, meaning "reply please" or "please respond". Do you want to go to the party?
Mr. Wang:	Yes. But I already have a plan for this Saturday. I don't know what I should

do about this invitation.

Henry: Well, it is fine to tell him that you can't go, and explain why.

Mr. Wang: I suppose I can change my plan, as I don't want to miss the chance to know more people.

Henry: If you plan to go, you should also tell him so. If you have a last-minute change, you should notify him as well.

Mr. Wang: Should I bring a plate or a box of chocolate?

Henry: No need. I guess Mr. Brown got everything organized. But it does say BYOB on the invitation. So if you want to drink beer, you need to bring it yourself. Otherwise, soft drink is provided.

Mr. Wang: I see. Thank you, Mr. White.

Henry: My pleasure, Mr. Wang.

Dialogue D   Invitation from Sophia

This is Mrs. Fanny Brown's first week in China and she's had no shortage of invitations from her new friends offering to take her out. Early in the morning the telephone rings.

Fanny: Hello, Fanny speaking.

Sophia: Morning, Fanny, this is Sophia. How are you?

Fanny: Fine, thank you.

Sophia: Have you got everything organized?

Fanny: Not yet. I'm trying to get everything sorted out in the flat. Cleaning, washing ... that sort of things.

Sophia: Do you need any help? I'm free until noon.

Fanny: You're very kind. But I can manage it myself. Anyhow, thank you all the same.

Sophia: I see. Well, I was wondering if you'd like to go to a concert on Thursday night. If I remember right, you did say you like classical music.

Fanny: Yes, that's right. It's nice of you to ask, Sophia, but I don't think I can go. Nancy has asked me to go to the theatre with her tomorrow night and she's got the tickets booked.

Sophia: Never mind. What about this weekend? This concert is still on then, I think.

Fanny: Great. What time does it start for Sunday?

Sophia: At 7 p.m.

Fanny: That'll be fine.

Sophia: Do you feel like going for a ride in the neighborhood by bike this Sunday?

Fanny: Oh，yes. That sounds great.

Sophia: How about we go at 9:30 in the morning. If we leave early we can cycle downtown. It's not far from here.

Fanny: That's great. But I can't go at 9:30，I'm afraid. I've arranged to meet one of my friends at 8 o'clock. Can we leave a bit later?

Sophia: OK. I'll be at your place at 10:30 then，alright?

Fanny: Yes. I look forward to it. See you on Sunday.

Sophia: By the way，have you got a bike?

Fanny: Yes. I've got one.

Sophia: That's fine. See you.

Fanny: See you.

Notes

1.	prospective host	邀请方
2.	initial	由单词首字母组成的缩写
3.	Hard Stone's	硬石酒吧
4.	draft	草稿
5.	high-rise	高层建筑
6.	The deadline is tomorrow.	明天是截止日。
7.	have fun	开心一下
8.	inspiration	灵感
9.	sparkle	如火花般闪现
10.	go Dutch	各付各的账单
11.	That's why you talked me into it.	这就是你把我骗去的原因吧。
12.	pick you up	开车接你
13.	California Red '89	(美国)加利福尼亚 89 年红酒
14.	Glad you could make it.	很高兴你能来。
15.	This is for you.	这是给你的礼物。
16.	a vintage	一瓶精品葡萄酒
17.	in a single specified year	只在那个特殊的一年中
18.	well furnished	家具齐全
19.	gorgeous decoration	靓丽的装饰
20.	Please make yourself at home.	请随便点。
21.	The air is refreshing.	空气新鲜。
22.	outdoor activity	户外运动

23. organize a barbecue	举行烧烤聚会
24. bring a plate	带菜(参加聚会)
25. BYOB(Bring Your Own Beer)	自带酒水
26. Get everything sorted out	整理东西
27. Cleaning, washing . . . that sort of thing.	打扫啦、洗衣啦等等这一类事情。
28. But I can manage it myself.	不过我自己能忙得过来。
29. anyhow	不管怎么说,总之
30. Never mind.	没关系,不用担心。
31. . . . we can cycle downtown.	……我们可以骑车去市中心。

 Functional Expressions

Inviting

1. Betty and I will throw a dinner party this weekend. We'd like you to come.

2. Come and see me next Friday.

3. Do join me for a coffee.

4. Don't you fancy coming along?

5. I'd very much like you to come to our dinner party.

6. If you could manage, we'd like you to attend our speech contest next week.

7. Shall we have a drink at this restaurant?

8. We'll be glad if you can come to attend our midterm meeting.

9. We're having a dance on Sunday. I hope you can make it.

10. We're having a party this weekend. Will you join us?

11. What about meeting my wife?

12. Why don't you come on a holiday with us?

13. Would you like to attend our wedding ceremony?

14. You are invited to our fancy dress party.

15. You must join us for lunch.

16. You will come to have dinner with us, won't you?

17. You'll be able to come, won't you?

Accepting an Invitation

1. Great, I'll count on it!

2. I won't say no!

3. I'd like nothing better.

4. I'd like to.

5. I'd love to!

6. I'll be a little late, is that OK?

7. I'll take you up on that.

8. I'm on for that! Thanks a lot.

9. It would be very nice to attend your wedding ceremony.

10. OK, if you insist.

11. OK.

12. Thank you. I'd like to very much.

13. That sounds a very nice idea.

14. That would be very nice.

15. With pleasure.

16. Yes, if you want me to.

17. Yes, if you'd like.

18. You bet!

Declining an Invitation

1. I wish I could, but David is coming this evening.

2. I'd like to, but my husband wouldn't like it.

3. I'd love to, but my father's going to call me at my place.

4. I'm afraid I can't. But thank you all the same.

5. I'm afraid I've already promised to meet Michael this evening.

6. I'm terribly sorry, but I don't think I can.

7. Much to my regret, but I wouldn't be able to attend your birthday party.

8. Thank you very much, but I'm already booked up for next Sunday.

9. That's very kind of you, but I have an appointment Friday evening.

 ## Communicative Task

Designing an Invitation Card

Types of Task: groups, class.

Functions Practiced: expressing certainty and uncertainty, partly agreeing, accepting invitation, declining invitation.

Pre-task

1. Suppose you are working for First Dial, a joint-venture mobile phone company. Your boss decides to invite some very important business partners to celebrate its 10th anniversary on the 25th of next month and asks you to make a sample of both the wording and the background pattern of

the invitation card. You must work on yourself in the design of the invitation card.

2. Some sample invitation cards（with words only）are illustrated below for your reference.

The Olympic Sailing Club

**Cordially Invites You
To Attend This
Annual Seaside Dinner
And Dance Party**

**On Saturday,
The Fourth August
2012
At Six O'clock
The Grand Hotel
118, Foothill Street
Qinhuangdao, Hebei
R.S.V.P.**

They finally got the house!

Please come and help
celebrate at a
Housewarming Party
for Kerry and Jamie
on Friday, July 6th, 2012
at 7:00 p.m.

276 Riverside Drive
Zhengzhou, Henan

B.Y.O.B.

Please be our guest

at the Grand Opening
of our new store
Gao & Gao's

Thursday,
May 31, 2012
from 5 until 8 p.m.
914 North Street
Wuhan, Hubei
(27) 62430132

Sarah and Susan Gao

Super Soccer Games

What's the next best thing
to being there?
Watching it
on a **super screen**!

RICHARD AND ANDREW
invite you
for a Super Soccer Party
Sunday, January 24

Pre-Game Party
Two o'clock at our dorm,
308, West Building

---

3. Notice the difference in formality and format when you begin your first adventure in invitation card designing in English.

4. Take your first sample invitation card to your group members and take turns to explain to them the purpose of the color, pattern, choice of words and the layout of the card and ask for their ideas about the improvement for your final copy.

5. Invite one of your classmates from another group to act as "your boss" for your group and try to persuade "your boss" to accept your work as the formal invitation card for the anniversary celebration.

6. Post your final version of the invitation card in a place in your classroom for exhibition.

Task Procedure

1. You and your group members now discuss what real party or event you'll hold next week or next month. It is better to have a true party or event for this task. Through this task, you will discover some words and expressions that you can use in your real life.

2. If you have no ideas about the party or event you can hold, choose one from the list below.

3. Discuss on how many of your fellow students will be invited to attend and celebrate for this special occasion.

4. Discuss who will be invited. To make your party or event a perfect one a proper guest list is important.

5. When you reach an agreement on the number of the guests and the list of names, it is the time to create your invitation card.

6. Now read the hints and tips on how to make invitation cards below before you get the ball rolling.

1) Try to keep the wording short, unambiguous and to the point.

2) Information and directions must be clear and precise.

3) Always make double check to avoid any disasters such as leaving out a vital piece of information!

7. Discuss the plan first in your group, for example, where and when you are planning for the occasion.

8. You and your group members now work together to design an invitation card template. Be careful about the location and date and, the most important thing, the wording.

9. When the template is done, use the Checklist below to ensure you've included every point.

10. Make copies for all invitees.

11. Use student ID numbers as phone numbers and make phone calls to the prospective

invitees and ask if they could show up for the occasion. If yes, deliver the card by yourself.

A List of Occasions and Events for Business & Individuals

academic seminars	anniversaries	back to school parties
birthdays	carnivals	charitable & formal events
engagement parties	family reunions	graduations
grand openings	Halloween parties	baby showers
holiday parties	housewarmings	moving or changes of address
New Year's parties	picnics	rehearsal dinners
retirements	sweet 19s	weddings
Over the Hill parties (a humorous birthday party for an elder person)		

A Checklist for Invitation Card

1. What is the purpose for the celebration?

2. Who is hosting the party or event?

3. Who is invited?

4. Where the party or event is held? Address details with directions if necessary.

5. Are Date and Time of the party or event specified?

6. Are there any special instructions you should include on the invitation? Bring a bottle, fancy dress, etc.

7. Is Reply and Contact information provided? Address or, if an informal invitation, telephone number or e-mail address.

8. Is the Date for reply included?

9. What is the way for invitees to reply, formal or informal?

10. If formal, a written reply should be required. Did you put RSVP at the end of the card?

Unit Ten

Food and Meal

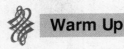

Warm Up

1. Say out Loud and Fast

1) Food plays a major role in any Chinese New Year celebration.

2) Red dishes are featured at weddings as red is the color of happiness in many Asian nations.

3) The Chinese word for pomelo sounds like the word "to have".

4) While nuts are high in calories, they are loaded with health benefits.

5) Here are some Chinese cooking tips on how to do most of the work ahead of time.

6) We got ten photo instructions showing how to make chili oil from dried chili peppers.

7) Eggs hold a special symbolic significance in many cultures, and China is no exception.

8) Baking instead of deep-frying reduces the fat and calories in this spicy Asian appetizer.

9) While the precise origins of chopsticks are unknown, they were definitely in use by the Shang dynasty from 1766 BC to 1122 BC.

10) Whether it's a festive New Year's celebration or a lazy summer brunch, dim sum is popular all year around.

2. Culture Tip

Western eating habits are very much different from those of our Chinese, just as seen in Western movies. Firstly, knife and fork are used to cut and pick up the food. Secondly, each person has his own plate of food. In a typical family setting, there will be some food served in the middle of the table. Usually, communal utensils are provided; so family members can use the shared utensils to place small portion of food on their own plates. You can't use your own knife or fork for the food served in the middle of the table. When you want to pick up food from your plate, use your fork, not your knife.

Meals are generally served in three courses. The first course is something small like a deviled egg, a cheese ball, an avocado and prawn cup or a small sea food salad to prepare you for eating. This is called an appetizer. The next one is the main course. It is the biggest and usually consists of meat and vegetable. For example, a lamb shank containing lamb, mashed potato, green beans and broccoli. Or a roasted beef served with roasted pumpkin, mushroom, carrot. The last one is the dessert which is usually a sweetmeat like cheese cakes, blueberry & apple jellies, mocha puddings, ice creams and such.

Generally speaking, table manners in English speaking nations are the same as those in China. For example, when you eat, eat quietly with your mouth closed. Conversation is allowed only after you've finished your food in your mouth. However, some behaviors are different. For instance, when you want to get something not in front of you, never reach over the table. You should ask someone to pass it to you by saying "Excuse me, could you pass me the salt?"

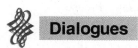 **Dialogues**

Dialogue A Dining Out

On Saturday evening, Richard White and Ying Xu decide to eat out. They come to the Friendship Restaurant near the Bund for dinner. An usherette is meeting them at the door.

Usherette: Good evening. Welcome to our restaurant. Have you booked a table?

Richard: No. But we'd like to have a table for two by the window, if possible.

Usherette: Let me check the booking record. Yes, sir, we have a table available but it's at the back of the restaurant. Is that OK with you?

Richard: What do you say, Ying?

Ying: It's fine with me.

Richard: OK, we'll take it.

(*The usherette leads them to a table and a waitress pours two cups of tea for them.*)

Waitress: Here's a cup of tea and the menu, sir. And another cup for you, Miss.

Richard: Do you have a menu in English? My Chinese isn't good enough to fully comprehend the menu.

Waitress: Certainly. Here is the English one.

Richard:	Well, I'm still not sure what some of these dishes are. Do you have any suggestions?
Waitress:	Do you like fish? The Sweet and Sour Fish is today's special. It tastes very nice. I'm sure you'll like it.
Richard:	That sounds good. Ying, how about this Sweet and Sour Fish?
Ying:	I had it before. It's appetizing. You should try it.
Waitress:	I also recommend the Kung Pao Chicken.
Richard:	I knew this one. I had it at City Wok when I was in the US. But I don't know how they cook it here. Is it very hot, I mean spicy? I'm not used to peppery food.
Waitress:	Yes, it is quite spicy. But I can ask the chef to make it mild if you like.
Ying:	Then I think you should try it. Taste the "authentic" Chinese food.
Richard:	(To waitress.) OK. We'll have the "real" Kung Pao Chicken. And a Yangchow Fried Rice.
Waitress:	What soup would you like?
Richard:	I feel like having a Wild Mushroom Soup. But I can't find it in the menu.
Waitress:	It's on the fifth page in the menu, sir.
Richard:	Oh, yes. I found it. Good, one big Wild Mushroom Soup. Please.
Waitress:	Any drinks?
Richard:	A glass of orange juice for the lady and a bottle of Tsingtao Beer for me, please.
Waitress:	OK. You ordered a Sweet and Sour Fish, a Kung Pao Chicken, mild, a Yangchow Fired Rice, a big Wild Mushroom Soup and an orange juice and a Tsingtao beer. Anything else?
Richard:	No, thanks. That's all to start with.
Waitress:	All right. Won't be long. Let me know if you need anything.
Richard:	OK, I will.

Dialogue B Breakfast at Home

It's time for breakfast. Richard enters into the kitchen to see if the breakfast is ready.

Richard:	Good morning, Mom.
Sophia:	Morning. What do you want to have for breakfast?
Richard:	I'll have two fried eggs, a toast and a cup of coffee, please.
Sophia:	The coffee is brewing. Take a seat. I'll fry the eggs for you.
Richard:	Thank you. Is Dad up?
Sophia:	He is in the shower. Oh, no, he's coming.

Henry: Morning.

Sophia: Good morning. You're going to have milk, aren't you?

Henry: Yes. I always have milk in the morning.

Sophia: What else are you going to have?

Henry: Just an English muffin. I had one yesterday, it was delicious.

Sophia: Do you want some fried eggs?

Henry: I'd rather have sausage this morning.

Sophia: Richard, here are the fried eggs and a toast for you. Coffee is ready. You may pour a cup yourself, and one cup for me if you don't mind. I'll fry the sausage for your father.

Richard: OK.

Henry: The fried eggs look good. Let me try a little.

Richard: There're two. You can have one if you like.

Henry: Thank you. (*Shouts towards the kitchen.*) Sophia, sorry I'll have some eggs, not the sausage, please. Eggs look more appetizing.

Sophia: OK, as you like. Sausage is nearly ready. I'll have the sausage myself then.

Richard: Dad, can you pass me the salt, please?

Henry: Here you are.

Richard: Thanks.

Sophia: (*Comes back from the kitchen.*) By the way, are you guys going to have supper at home?

Richard: No. I'll go to Hugh's home to join his birthday party with Ying tonight.

Henry: I'll be home for supper.

Sophia: Shall we have beef steak for supper?

Henry: Beef steak again? We had it yesterday and the day before yesterday. How about fish? A cod, a cod with pickled vegetable.

Sophia: I like cod with pickled vegetable, too. But I don't know how to cook it. Then how about having our dinner at the Park Hotel tonight?

Henry: I couldn't agree more.

Richard: Dining in the Park Hotel without me again? How disappointed I am, you know?

Dialogue C   A Business Lunch

Mr. White invites his client, Mr. Jiede Gao, to a nearby restaurant to have a business lunch together. Mr. Gao seems very happy with the lunch and also quite confident about his first purchase.

Mr. Gao:	That was a wonderful meal, Mr. White. It seems you are a regular visitor here. All the staff appears to know you very well.
Henry:	I'm glad you enjoyed it. Yes, it's a good place and close to the office. I come here quite often. The food here is usually of a pretty high quality.
Mr. Gao:	Especially, the paper-wrapped chicken and the sour-pepper soup.
Henry:	Would you like a drink? A brandy, perhaps?
Mr. Gao:	That would be very pleasant.
Henry:	Two brandies please, waiter.
Waiter:	Certainly, sir.
Henry:	Now perhaps we should return to business. Just then in my office you were asking if there could be any discount on the computers. How many sets are you planning to purchase?
Mr. Gao:	Our factory would like to buy 65 sets of the model K7M - 1 as the first purchase. Then maybe 20 sets of the ZF - 200 and about 5 sets of the M2 server afterwards.
Henry:	In this case, we can give you a discount of five per cent.
Mr. Gao:	I think a discount of ten per cent would be more appealing.
Henry:	Since you are ordering a large quantity, and more to come, I could give you an eight per cent discount.
Mr. Gao:	Can't you just take the other two per cent off?
Henry:	Sorry, that's the best I can do for the price. But I can extend the warranty to two years for free.
Mr. Gao:	OK. I'll take it. Here's to our first business deal! (*Raises his glass.*)
Henry:	And more to come.
Mr. Gao:	When will the computers be shipped to our factory?
Henry:	We'll ship them as soon as we get the deposit. If by air, it'll probably take two days, but the shipping cost is a bit higher. If by surface, may be two weeks.
Mr. Gao:	By air, please. We'll pay the delivery. We need the computers urgently. Thank you, Mr. White. And thank you for the lunch, too.
Henry:	You are welcome. I'll see you again soon, right?
Mr. Gao:	That's for sure. I'll probably come back for the second shipment in two months.
Henry:	See you then, Mr. Gao.
Mr. Gao:	See you. Bye.
Henry:	Take care.

Dialogue D   Dinner at Park Hotel

Mr. Henry White and his wife are having dinner with Henry's old classmate, Dan Jackson, in the Park Hotel.

Henry:	Shall we try some Chinese wines and spirits tonight? They have Mao Tai and a wine called Dynasty. Mao Tai is a famous distilled spirit with a long history in China.
Dan:	They told me Mao Tai is very strong, isn't it?
Henry:	Yes, but this kind of Mao Tai isn't very strong. It tastes mild and won't give you a bad hangover. Would you like to try it?
Dan:	OK. I'll try a little.
Henry:	Let's drink to our career in Shanghai and to our health.
Dan:	And to our families.
Sophia:	Cheers!
Henry:	Now help yourself to this dish. This is pork and has been cooked twice. A special way to cook pork in southern China. It's palatable.
Dan:	Very savory. You seem to know a lot about Chinese food.
Henry:	Yes, indeed. We're accustomed to the food here. We've stayed here much longer than you. You'll be used to Chinese food soon after.
Dan:	Generally speaking, I like Chinese food, but some dishes are just too oily. They don't agree with me at all. Besides, I'm afraid I'm gaining weight.
Sophia:	Dan, try steamed crabs. It tastes best while it's warm. Crab is full of protein, not fat.
Dan:	Yum! Fresh and delicious. Where did the crabs come from?
Henry:	From a lake called Yangcheng in Jiangsu Province, about 80 kilometers from Shanghai. They are the best in China. Chinese people like them very much and always have them with the dip of ginger and vinegar.
Dan:	The dip is also tasty. I like the flavor.
Sophia:	Here comes the Peking Roast Duck. Dan, please get a piece of steamed pancake, put some duck meat, some scallions on the top, and then add some sweet bean sauce to ensure the classic Chinese taste. You can also add some cucumber sticks if you like. Then wrap it up and eat with hands.
Dan:	What a nice color and flavor! It is luscious!
Henry:	It's a prestigious northern dish. Would you like some more?
Dan:	No, thank you. I'm just fine.
Sophia:	Try these strawberries, Dan.
Dan:	They are sweet and juicy. I must say this was a wonderful and lovely meal.

Henry: I'm glad you enjoyed it.

Dan: Thank you for inviting me and thank you again for the meal.

Henry: It's our pleasure.

Notes

1. communal utensils 共用餐具
2. generally served in three courses 一般要分三次上菜
3. a deviled egg 魔鬼蛋(抹蛋黄酱与芥末的煮鸡蛋)
4. an avocado and prawn cup 一杯油梨虾仁小吃
5. appetizer 开胃菜
6. mashed potato 土豆泥
7. lamb shank (烤)羊膝
8. blueberry & apple jellies 蓝莓苹果冻
9. mocha puddings 摩卡布丁
10. table manner 餐桌礼仪
11. the Bund (上海)外滩
12. the booking record 预约登记簿
13. Let's take the table. 我们就坐那个餐桌吧。
14. The Sweet and Sour Fish is today's special. 今天糖醋鱼特价。
15. Kung Pao Chicken 宫保鸡丁
16. authentic 正宗的,真实的
17. Yangchow Fried Rice 扬州炒饭
18. City Wok 一家在美国加利福尼亚州的中餐馆
19. Is it very hot? 很辣吗?
20. toast 烤面包片
21. English muffin 英式小松糕(饼)
22. a cod with pickled vegetable 酸菜鳕鱼
23. purchase price 进货价格
24. a regular visitor 常客
25. paper-wrapped chicken 纸包鸡
26. a discount of five per cent 百分之五折扣
27. by air 航空运输
28. by surface 海陆路运输
29. Here's to ... 为……干杯
30. Park Hotel 上海国际饭店
31. give you a bad hangover 让你喝醉

32. palatable	美味可口
33. Very savory.	非常好吃。
34. They don't agree with me at all.	它们一点儿也不合我的胃口。
35. I'm gaining weight.	我要发胖了。
36. Yum!	真好吃啊！（拟声词）
37. dip	蘸汁，调料
38. Peking Roast Duck	北京烤鸭
39. steamed pancake	荷叶饼
40. scallion	香葱
41. It is luscious.	真是又香又好吃啊！

 ## Functional Expressions

Presenting Something to Somebody

1. A hamburger for you, Judy.

2. Allow me to present you with a small token of the company's gratitude for your twenty years' service.

3. Can I give you a copy of today's *China Daily*?

4. Here's the report you need.

5. I want you to have this.

6. I'd like to give you this brooch.

7. I'd like you to have these pair of shoes.

8. Need the saucepan?

9. This is Susan's letter to you.

10. This T-shirt is for you, George.

11. Want the hammer?

Offering to Do Something for Somebody

1. Any point in my painting the room for you?

2. Anything I can do to help?

3. Can I give you a hand with the dishes?

4. Can I help you out with some money?

5. Give me a ring whenever you're in trouble.

6. How about if I get some paper for you?

7. If you like, I could make you a suit.

8. If you want, I could heat it up for you.

9. I'll bring you some flowers.

10. I'll give you a hand with the dishes.

11. Is there anything I can do?

12. Just call me if you need any help.

13. Let me get it for you.

14. Let me know if you want any support.

15. May I be of any assistance?

16. May I help you in with those bags?

17. Might I help at all?

18. Need some help, Winifred?

19. Shall I help you into your coat?

20. Want a hand?

21. What can I do to help prepare the dinner?

22. Why don't you let me help?

23. Would you like any help?

24. Would you like me to fix some coffee?

25. Would you want me to help you with that?

Accepting an Offer of Help

1. Great!

2. If you're sure it's no trouble for you.

3. Just what I needed!

4. Oh, would you? Thanks.

5. Thank you, I'd appreciate it.

6. That'd be a big help. Thanks a lot.

7. That's nice of you, thank you.

8. That's very kind of you, thanks.

9. Yes, please.

Declining an Offer of Help

1. I don't think so, thank you.

2. It's very good of you to offer, but I can call a taxi.

3. No, don't bother, I can do it myself.

4. No, it's all right. I can manage.

5. No, it's OK, thanks.

6. No, thank you.

7. Please don't bother. I can manage it myself.

8. Please don't trouble yourself about it.

9. Thank you for your offer, but I can manage.

10. Thanks a lot, but I'm OK.

11. That's very kind of you, but I'm expecting my wife.

Communicative Task

Food Mart on Hand

Types of Task: pair, group, class.

Functions Practiced: stating you are able to do something, asking for help, calling out food names, offering to help.

Pre-task

1. Read the two recipes attached below in order to be familiar with the ingredients and terms used in preparing and cooking food. You may need a dictionary at this stage.

Recipes

A. Crisp-skin Chicken

Ingredients:

1 chicken (1 1/2 kg)	1 tbsp. vinegar
2 tbsp. soy sauce	2 tbsp. honey
1 tbsp. cooking wine	1 tsp. brown sugar
2 tbsp. all-purpose flour	1 tsp. salt
1/2 kg peanut oil for deep-frying	

Method:

1) Put the chicken in a large saucepan and add boiling water halfway up the sides of the chicken.

2) Cover tightly and simmer until just tender, about 45 minutes to 1 hour.

3) Drain, rinse under cold water and dry with kitchen paper.

4) Mix the vinegar, soy sauce, honey, cooking wine and sugar. Brush this mixture all over the chicken and then hang the chicken in an airy place to dry, for about 30 minutes.

5) Brush over the remaining soy sauce mixture and hang again for another 20～30 minutes.

6) Mix the flour and salt together and rub well into the chicken skin.

7) Heat peanut oil until very hot in a wok. Fry the chicken in the oil until golden and crisp.

8) Drain well on absorbent kitchen paper.

9) Chop the chicken into 8 pieces.

10) Serve warm with a salt and pepper dip.

B. Diced Chicken with Fried Chestnuts

Ingredients：

1 1/2 kg chicken	4 dried mushrooms
15 shelled chestnuts	1/3 cup oil
1 tsp. starch	1 tbsp. cooking wine
2 tbsp. soy sauce	1 tsp. salt
1 tsp. brown sugar	

Method：

1) Soak the mushrooms in hot water for 10 minutes.

2) Cut the chestnuts in half and fry in 2 tablespoons of the oil for 2 minutes. Drain on absorbent kitchen paper to remove all traces of oil.

3) Cut the chicken meat into small pieces, fry in the remaining oil for 3 minutes over a fierce heat, stirring all the time.

4) Mix the starch into a smooth paste with the cooking wine, soy sauce, salt and sugar. Add to the chicken and mix well.

5) Drain the mushrooms and chop roughly, add to the pan and cook for 2 minutes. Add the chestnuts.

tbsp. = tablespoon 汤匙	tsp. = teaspoon 茶匙
teaspoonful 一茶匙量	all-purpose flour 中筋面粉

2. Now recall two dishes you or your mother once cooked on a special occasion. For example, your father's birthday, the New Year's eve, Spring Festival family reunion, or farewell parties.

3. On your own notepad, write down the cooking method of the dishes, including the necessary ingredients and procedures. Here are some popular Chinese foods for your reference：

Sweet and Sour Pork Spareribs	Chicken Fried Rice
Beef with Broccoli	Egg Drop Soup
Hot and Sour Soup	Spring Roll
Sweet and Sour Chicken	Four Happiness Meatballs
Cashew Chicken（腰果鸡块）	Stir-fried Beef
Kung Pao Chicken	Tea Eggs
Chow Mein（炒面）	Sesame Seed Balls（麻球）

4. Your group is going to have a weekend dinner party and decides to offer the guests the best dish that each of you has ever cooked. So now, take turns to tell your group the

delicious food you are going to offer at the weekend party and give a detailed report of the ingredients used and steps for cooking.

5. If you have never cooked a dish by yourself, turn to your group members for help.

6. Come back to your own desk now and prepare 12 labeling cards (or sheets of paper) in size of 4 cm × 6 cm.

7. Label one food, drink or dish ingredient item (e. g., Hot and Sour Soup, orange juice, vinegar, salt, pepper, etc.) on each card. The ingredient items on your cards should be the ones in your reported dishes.

Task Procedure

1. Read all the steps in this task first and make sure you know all the rules. Discuss them with your pair if necessary.

2. Now bring your prepared cards to your group. Food, drink and dish ingredient items on your labeled cards represent the commodities that you want to sell. The purpose of this game is to see who in your group will be the first one to sell out all his/her goods.

3. Offer your help if your partner has trouble writing out the food items.

4. You and your other group members sit around a desk. Put together the cards that all your group members brought with.

5. Add one more card with the label "First Player".

6. Remember the way you play poker? You will play this game in a similar way you play poker. Now shuffle and deal out the cards equally to each member in the group and leave the last card on the table.

7. The one who got the card labeled "First Player" puts the "First Player" card aside, takes the last card on the table, and then starts the game by bringing her/his first card out on the desk (Begin to sell your goods).

8. The person sits next to the first player on the left will be the second one to play. However, she/he has to obey the following rules:

Rule 1: This sales game should be played in an ascendant alphabetical order. In other words, the letter "a" is on the bottom level while the letter "z" is on the top level. For example, if the first player bring out a card labeled "salt", the second player can only choose from her/his set a card named "vinegar", not the one with the word "pepper" because the beginning letter "v" is on the higher level than the letter "s". Nevertheless, the second player can put down the card with the word "sausage", since the third letter in the word "sausage" is "u", though the first two letters are the same in two words, "salt" and "sausage".

Rule 2: Each round ends when no one could bring out any card with the letters on higher level. The last player wins the first round and then he/she starts out the next round.

Rule 3：The winner will be the one who has bought out all the cards first，which means the winner has sold out all the goods.

9. Now you know how this task goes. Try it and good luck to you.

10. The winners of every group should introduce her/his dishes to class with a brief description of the cooking steps.

Unit Eleven

Shopping

 Warm Up

1. Say out Loud and Fast

1) Does Sale really mean Sale? According to retail gurus, not always.

2) Many rebate redemption rules are designed to frustrate consumers into giving up getting their money back.

3) The internet is also a magnet for thieves who want to defraud people out of money.

4) Online consumers enjoy the conveniences and broad selection of merchandise, services and information available online.

5) Over 69 percent of shoppers haggled for a better price in 2010. Do you have a successful "Haggle" story to share?

6) If you are looking for inexpensive Halloween costumes and decorations, this is a good place to start.

7) Yugster.com is a popular — one deal a day — website offering low prices on a variety of products.

8) Getting a good bargain on a new set of luggage is not all about getting the cheapest price.

9) Did you know it is not illegal for retailers to charge different prices on identical products to different people?

10) I hate shopping, especially when I know little about the real wants of the person I'm shopping for.

2. Culture Tip

While you are shopping in the United States, you will discover that prices vary considerably from store to store and from time to time. Almost every store has its own "special days" during some important occasions, such as a store's anniversary, statutory and local holidays, and even long weekends, to lure people to buy things at reduced prices.

Some Americans who are not so well-off often shop at "discount stores" or "thrift shops", which you may also find interesting. The purchase of used, second-hand clothing, furniture and other household articles may be a lash-up for those who are short of money and want to start up their independent life immediately.

Clothing sizes are measured differently in the US from the way they're measured in countries where the metric system is used.

Women's Size

	Blouse/Dresses/Suits	Shoes
USA	8, 10, 12, 14, 16, 18	6, 7, 8, 9
Metric	38, 40, 42, 44, 46, 48	37, 38, 40, 41

Men's Size

	Suits	Shirts	Shoes
USA	36, 38, 40, 42, 44	15, 16, 17, 18	6, 7, 8, 9, 10
Metric	46, 48, 50, 52, 54	38, 41, 43, 45	39, 41, 42, 43, 44

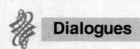

Dialogues

Dialogue A   Christmas Shopping

Christmas is drawing near. Mrs. Sophia White is doing her Christmas shopping. Then she runs into Mrs. Helen King, her colleague and friend.

Helen: Hi, Sophia.

Sophia: Hi, Helen. What are you doing?

Helen: We are going back to America for Christmas next week. I want to buy some local Chinese specialties as Christmas gifts for my family and friends at home.

Sophia: Good idea. I think you should go to the Arts & Crafts Store. You can find various traditional Chinese goods there.

Helen: Really? Thank you for your advice.

Sophia: My pleasure. Have a nice day!

Helen:	Thank you. You too!
	(*In the Arts & Crafts Store.*)
Tony:	Good morning, Ma'am. I'm Tony. May I help you?
Helen:	Oh, yes. I want to buy some Christmas presents for my family and some friends. But there are so many wonderful things here that I actually don't know how to make a choice. Could you suggest something?
Tony:	Certainly! Please have a look at these unique Chinese fans. They are made of sandalwood with natural fragrance. You can find different paintings on different fans. Look! There are some ancient Chinese ladies playing in a garden on this one.
Helen:	Let me have a look. Dear me! Is it cool? And it's got such a gorgeous aroma!
Tony:	Yes. It's a good gift for ladies. And it isn't expensive at all. It only costs twenty *yuan*.
Helen:	Well, I'll take ten, please. I'll give them to my friends. I'm sure they'll be crazy about them. Oh, that vase also looks great. May I have a close look?
Tony:	Sure! That is a fine piece of work. It's a cloisonné vase which flourished in the Ming Dynasty. And it is actually a copy of the palace crafts.
Helen:	How quaint! I'm sure my parents love it. How much is it?
Tony:	Four hundred and twenty *yuan* each.
Helen:	I'll take two then. One for my parents, and the other for myself. I will put it in our living room.
Tony:	Yes. Chinese people always put them in the living room or study.
Helen:	It must be great. Thank you for help. How much are they in all?
Tony:	Ten sandalwood fans. Two hundred. Two vases ... er ... that's eight hundred and forty. In total, one thousand and forty *yuan*, please.
Helen:	Here you are, eleven hundred.
Tony:	Thank you. Here is the change. Have a nice day!
Helen:	Bye!

Dialogue B   At a Department Store

Mrs. Sophia White is shopping at a department store. She wants to buy a sweater for Richard. Xiaofang Qin, the shop assistant, walks up to Sophia.

| Xiaofang: | What can I do for you, Madam? |
| Sophia: | I want to buy a sweater for my son. May I look at that one? |

Xiaofang:	Sure. This V-neck cashmere sweater is of high quality. You see, it is soft and warm. This brand is very famous in China. And the style is quite fashionable.
Sophia:	It looks really nice. But I don't like black. Are there any other colors?
Xiaofang:	Yes. There are dark blue, light yellow... what about silver gray? It's rather popular this year.
Sophia:	That looks smart! But it's over the budget, I guess.
Xiaofang:	The normal price is 780 *yuan*. Now, we have Christmas sale in our department store. You can take 20 percent off the original price. So now it's only 624 *yuan*.
Sophia:	It's a real bargain! I'll get one.
Xiaofang:	What size sweater do you think would your son wear?
Sophia:	Extra large.
Xiaofang:	I see. Here you are. An extra large silver gray V-neck cashmere sweater. Madam, do you need anything else?
Sophia:	Can I please have a look at that T-shirt with the image of panda on?
Xiaofang:	Sure. It's one hundred percent cotton. Panda is the symbol of China. Many foreign tourists like them very much.
Sophia:	It's lovely. I'll take four of them, two large, one medium, and one small. How much are they?
Xiaofang:	35 *yuan* each.
Sophia:	Can I pay by credit card?
Xiaofang:	Sure, please pay at the cashier desk over there. I'll pack them for you.

Dialogue C   On-line Shopping

Richard, who frequently shops online, has never been so impatient for his parcels as he is now. He has been counting every day while he is waiting for the goods he ordered to arrive, as many deliveries have been delayed over the past month.

Sophia:	You look nervous, Richard. Are you all right?
Richard:	To tell you the truth, I'm on pins and needles.
Sophia:	What's up?
Richard:	I ordered several stuffs on Taobao. com. Normally it takes only three days to deliver the parcel, but this time ten days passed, I still haven't got it.
Sophia:	Have you contacted the seller?
Richard:	Yes. I saw many sellers on Taobao. com have posted apologetic announcements to customers for the delays in delivery. It says "Many

parcels are still at the airports and cannot be delivered on time."

Sophia: Who should be blamed for, the sellers or the express delivery companies?

Richard: It is mainly caused by a big increase of online shopping orders because of discounts offered by e-commerce companies at the end of the year.

Sophia: And the bad weather makes things worse, I guess.

Richard: Yeah. Major express delivery companies in China have put up notices saying they are gearing up to cope with the delay in recent days.

Sophia: It seems on-line shopping is risky. Why not go to a store?

Richard: I am used to e-shopping and take advantage of low prices online and the expanding logistics network across the country. Who wants to go to a store while there are so many options and a rather low price offered online?

Sophia: Is it complicated to shop online?

Richard: Not at all! First, open a bank account which allows you to pay online. You could choose a bank like ICBC or Bank of China, etc. Second, select an online store or an e-shopping website to register an account. Third, login to the website and search your favorite goods. If you want to buy, click the button "purchase" on the website.

Sophia: Sounds easy! But how do you pay? Online, too?

Richard: For the payment, simply select "pay by e-bank". Then your money will be transferred from your account to "Alipay" — a payment platform between the buyer and seller.

Sophia: Then?

Richard: Wait for the seller to deliver the goods you ordered. Usually, it takes two or three days to receive the goods.

Sophia: How can I be assured my money wouldn't be cheated?

Richard: Check upon the delivery sent by the seller after you received it immediately. If there is no mistake or no quality problem, then click the feed back button "OK" on the payment webpage, which gives your permission to "Alipay" to complete the transaction. If the goods have any problem, you could make a complaint first and then send the goods back to the seller. Your money will be returned from "Alipay". Mom, do you want me to open an account for you?

Sophia: Well, er... after you've received your parcel.

Dialogue D   At the Green Grocer's

Mrs. Sophia White is going to throw a party at home tonight. Ying Xu comes to help her. Now they are in a convenience green grocer's in their neighborhood.

Sophia:	This place is different from a supermarket，isn't it? I don't come here very often because I think the prices are higher than at a supermarket.
Ying:	Yeah. There isn't much choice，either. I mean there are only one or two brands of each kind of goods，but that makes choosing easier.
Sophia:	When I'm not in a hurry，I usually enjoy comparing brands and prices so I can get the most for my money.
Ying:	Why don't you go to the farmers' markets? They do very good business. There are vegetables，fruits and meat and they are all fresh and reasonably-priced. There's also an advantage to shop there，that is，you can bargain with the sellers.
Sophia:	But that is exactly the disadvantage for me! When the sellers see a foreign face like me，they usually offer higher prices. So I'd better shop at a supermarket.
Ying:	(*Speaking to the shop assistant*.) I'm surprised at your milk prices. Your prices are competitive with the large chains. How do you do it?
Shop assistant:	The prices are low only on selected items. We can't really compete with those supermarkets，but at least there are no long queues. And this is probably the only place open at night in this neighborhood.
Sophia:	Pardon me. Where can I find Tsingtao beer?
Shop assistant:	It's in Aisle Six.
Sophia:	Thank you. (*After a while*.) Fish，minced pork，broccoli，potatoes，onions，beer，bananas ... I've got all I need except for a bottle of Japanese soy sauce and a bottle of Chinese vinegar. Where do you keep them，Miss?
Ying:	They're on the shelf right behind you.
Shop assistant:	Yes, they are on this shelf. We've got — Japanese soy sauce Tamari，Koikuchi，and a Japanese popular barbecue sauce Teriyaki，too. In fact，we have almost all Asian sauces and pastes in store，from Chinese Dou Ban Jiang，Shrimp Paste to Hoi Sin Sauce，from Laochou to Oyster Sauce，and we also have Gochujang from Korea and Sriracha Sauce from Thai.
Sophia:	Oh, I didn't look this way... Yes，you seem to have a big pile of stuff here. Good，all are my favorite brands. Oh，yes. I also need some cabbage for soup. Do you have any today?
Shop assistant:	I'm sorry. Cabbage is out of stock at the moment.
Sophia:	Oh，that's too bad. Will you get some in today?
Shop assistant:	We're expecting to get a new stock in this afternoon. You can come back again after noon.
Sophia:	I'm afraid I'm not free then. OK. I'll get some carrots instead. Here we are.

	How much are they altogether?
Shop assistant：	232 *yuan* in all. Will there be anything else?
Sophia：	No，thank you.
Shop assistant：	Cash or card?
Sophia：	I pay cash. Two hundred and forty.
Shop assistant：	Here is the change. Have a nice day!

Notes

1.	statutory holidays	法定假日
2.	lash-up	应急方案；临时拼凑的东西
3.	run into	偶尔遇到
4.	local specialties	土特产
5.	the Arts & Crafts Store	工艺美术品商店
6.	sandalwood	檀香木
7.	a gorgeous aroma	浓郁的香味
8.	a cloisonné vase	景泰蓝花瓶
9.	the palace crafts	宫廷工艺品
10.	How quaint!	多么精致古雅啊！
11.	V-neck cashmere sweater	鸡心领羊绒（开司米）毛衣
12.	It's a real bargain!	很合算！
13.	It's one hundred percent cotton.	这是百分之百的纯棉。
14.	cashier desk	收银台
15.	on pins and needles	坐立不安
16.	express delivery company	快递公司
17.	gear up	加快
18.	logistics	物流
19.	register	注册
20.	Alipay	支付宝
21.	check upon the delivery	验货
22.	a green grocery	蔬菜水果店
23.	throw a party	请客吃饭
24.	minced pork	猪肉馅
25.	soy sauce	酱油
26.	Tamari	日本黑酱油（不含小麦的纯大豆酱油）
27.	Koikuchi	日本普通酱油
28.	Teriyaki	日本照烧汁（烧烤酱）

29. Asian sauces and pastes	亚洲酱汁类料理
30. Dou Ban Jiang, Shrimp Paste	豆瓣酱,虾酱
31. Hoi Sin Sauce	海鲜酱(中国)
32. from Laochou to Oyster Sauce	从老抽到耗油
33. Gochujang from Korea	韩国辣椒酱
34. Sriracha Sauce from Thai	泰国斯里拉查香甜辣椒酱
35. out of stock at the moment	暂时无货

 Functional Expressions

Asking for Information

1. Any clue what's happened?

2. Can you tell me something about it?

3. Could anyone tell me who was here a moment ago?

4. Could you tell me some more about it?

5. Do you happen to know his name?

6. Do you happen to know what time the film begins?

7. Do you work in a bank, if you don't mind me asking?

8. Excuse me, do you know how to play bridge?

9. Excuse me, do you know why the bus is late?

10. Got any idea how to turn on the air conditioner?

11. I hope you don't mind me asking, but I wonder whether you could tell me when the train for Newcastle leaves.

12. I'd like to know more about the new product.

13. I'd appreciate if you could tell me where you're going next week.

14. Is he going abroad, do you know?

15. Something else I'd like to know is which team won the final.

16. Sorry to keep after you, but could you tell me who's responsible for it?

17. Sorry to trouble you, but will he come here tomorrow?

18. Would you kindly tell me whose house was broken into?

19. Would you mind telling me how the car stuck the lamp post?

Asking if Somebody Knows Something

1. Could you give me any information on how to operate the recorder?

2. Did someone tell you about the robbery yesterday?

3. Did you hear what happened to Julia?

4. Do you happen to know anything about the TV program for tonight?

5. Do you know about the recent drought in Afghanistan?

6. Do you know anything about the history of Egypt?

7. Has somebody told you about their divorce?

8. Have you any idea how high the Oriental Pearl TV Tower is?

9. Have you heard about the story of Lei Feng?

10. Know anything about the computer virus?

11. You know about our goals, don't you?

Expressing Knowledge of Something

1. For all I know, you can't get any dictionaries in this bookstore.

2. Guess what: they fell into a fight in the street yesterday.

3. I hear Mr. Robinson is going to resign.

4. I've been told they are going to be on sale this weekend.

5. Most married people fall out over money, you know?

6. So I hear.

7. So, I'm told. But thank you for telling me this.

8. So, Carol said.

9. That's what I heard.

10. Yes, I do know she's leaving for good.

11. Yes, I've heard about the news.

Expressing Ignorance of Something

1. Don't ask me the price of VCD player. I don't even have a TV.

2. Haven't a clue.

3. I don't know how to start a motorcycle.

4. I don't know the first thing about the flea market in this neighborhood.

5. I don't know where you can buy a new typewriter, I'm afraid.

6. I haven't got the faintest idea about her crimes.

7. I wish I knew.

8. I'm afraid I can't help you there.

9. I'm afraid I've no idea whether it is safe to sail in this weather.

10. I'm quite in the dark about it.

11. I'm sorry I don't know when they made the arrangements.

12. I've got no idea.

13. Search me.

14. Sorry, I don't know.

15. Sorry, I really don't know.

16. Sorry, no idea.

17. That's news to me.

Communicative Task

Classroom Mini-mart

Types of Task: pair, class.

Functions Practiced: asking for information, asking if somebody knows something, reading prices, bargaining on a deal, expressing ignorance of something.

Pre-task

1. Work together with your pair to read the information for the task.

1) The task is to buy and sell commodities in Classroom Mini-mart.

2) The roles in this task are a General Manager of Classroom Mini-mart, shop assistants (6~12 persons), referees (5 persons), and shoppers.

3) The General Manager is granted the full authority to run the store, including the commodities, the quantity, the price, hiring the shop assistants, and deciding the layout and setting of the store.

4) The duty of the referees is to work together to prepare a ten-item shopping list for each shopper according to the commodities available in the Classroom Mini-mart. The items on each list should be different and the description should be as detailed as possible. For example, not just toothpaste, but a MAXIM (brand name) toothpaste. Some commodities even need a more detailed specification, for example, A4 photocopy paper. When Classroom Mini-mart closes, referees will decide who THE CRAZIEST SHOPPER is.

5) The duty of the shop assistants is to help the General Manager to make price tags during the preparing period and sell the goods when Classroom Mini-mart opens. Each assistant is in change of selling one particular category of commodity. At the end of the task, the General Manager, according to the number of sales (the number of costumers she/he receives) and the number of mistakes made in calculating the amount of money, will give the title of THE MOST VALUEBLE BUSINESSPERSON to one of the assistants.

6) The shoppers should receive the shopping list randomly given by referees and then buy the assigned goods in Classroom Mini-mart when it opens. The winner is the one who bought all the items on her/his list and no mistakes were made during the shopping mission.

2. If you are lucky to be named the General Manager of Classroom Mini-mart by your classmates, here are some hints for you:

1) Get 6 to 12 (depending on the size of your class) of your classmates to be your shop assistants and assign them different roles in Classroom Mini-mart.

2) Rearrange the back part of the classroom so that it looks like a store. A simple way to do it is to line up four desks against the back wall and place two chairs on each desk. These desks and chairs will be used as commodity display shelves. Put another row of four desks next to the display shelves with a space of one meter in between. These desks will be used as counters in the sales activities. Your shop assistants will stand between the two rows of desks when they sell stuff for you.

3) Classroom Mini-mart should sell at least the following commodities:

a. books, newspapers and magazines

b. food and kitchen utensils

c. bedding and bathroom articles

d. stationery

e. furniture

f. computers and cell phones

4) Discuss with your shop assistants the items in the above categories and ask them to write out price tags (see the sample price tags below). Put these price tags on the display shelves instead of real goods you want to sell.

Sample: Price tag 1

> **Commodity:** DVD player
> **Original:** Germany
> **Price/Unit:** 430 *yuan*

Sample: Price tag 2

> **Commodity:** Can opener
> **Original:** China
> **Price/Unit:** 38.60 RMB

3. If you are going to play the role of a customer, you need to make some personal checks as a form of payment to buy goods in Classroom Mini-mart. Notice the italicized words in the check below were written by a customer, Wang Dawei, when he was shopping in Hua Lian Supermarket, 19 May, 2010.

Sample: Personal Check

> **The Student Bank of China**
> 1126, Xueqing Street
> Beijing, 100083
>
> Date *19 May 2010*
>
> Pay *Hua Lian Supermarket*
> in the order of *Twelve yuan*
> *and Ninety-nine Cents only*   ¥ *12.99*
>
>   Signature *Wang Dawei*
> Check No. P272956   Account No. DM9537581

4. After all students finish reading, hold a class meeting to assign the roles for everyone

in class.

5. Get everything ready for the selling and shopping activities, for example, holding a management meeting, setting up Classroom Mini-mart, making tags, shopping lists and checks, etc.

Task Procedure

1. Now the Classroom Mini-mart opens and it will be opening for thirty minutes only.

2. As a customer, you need rush into the mart and buy what you have to buy on your shopping list.

3. If you are the assistant in the mart, make sure to record every sale for every item and receive the checks with the correct amount of money and the signature from the right person. Hand the sale record and the check to your General Manager as soon as you have finished one single sale.

4. The General Manager collects the received checks and sales records from the assistants, and reports them to referees.

5. The referees will calculate the shopping records for every customer.

6. When the Classroom Mini-mart closes, hold a celebrating party in class to announce the winners of **THE CRAZIEST SHOPPER** and **THE MOST VALUABLE BUSINESSPERSON**.

Unit Twelve

On the Way

 **Warm Up**

1. Say out Loud and Fast

1) Excuse me. I'm looking for the nearest agency selling Amtrak railway tickets. Is it located in that tallest blue building on the south of the river?

2) Do you offer any economical ways to discover the sights and attractions on both sides of the US/Canada border?

3) Many accidents happen to cyclists because car drivers cannot see them until it is too late to stop.

4) In major cities, our company-operated terminals provide full-service ticketing and package express service, with extensive hours of operation.

5) Some of our bus stops may be at a local airport or transit center, while others may simply be a stop along a highway route, without an enclosed waiting area.

6) For those within Mexico who wish to travel by our service, our subsidiary Sunny Tour can be your best choice.

7) By the way, should I take bus 505 or 609 to Discovery Science & Technology Centre at Line 8 subway station on High Street?

8) Sorry to disturb you, but I am wondering which bus I should take to Life Adventure Park. Could you show me the route on the map?

9) The road environment still represents the single highest cause of death and injury to young people in Scotland.

10) Founded in 1914, Greyhound Lines, Inc. is the largest provider of intercity bus transportation, serving more than 2,300 destinations with 13,000 daily departures across North America.

2. Culture Tip

In many cities in the United States buses have letters and/or numbers indicating their routes. Usually the exact fare is required because you can't get change on a bus.

There are subway systems in several cities. New York City has an extensive and rather complicated rapid transit system. Each train is designated by a letter or a number. It's important to remember that you must have a token or, in some cases, the exact charge to get on the platforms.

In the United Kingdom, however, the subway systems are usually known by some other names such as the Underground or Tube in London and the Metro in Newcastle. A subway in the United Kingdom is a tunnel under a road where people can cross the road safely.

（Tokens，New York City 美国纽约乘地铁用代金硬币）

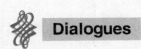 **Dialogues**

Dialogue A   A Lift

Richard has an appointment with a client at a Cafe on Long Street. David Smith, one of his colleagues, offers him a lift.

Richard： What's the time by your watch, David?

David： It's ten to five. Why?

Richard： I've got an appointment with a client. I'm gonna meet him in the city at 5:30. I'm afraid I'll be late.

David： Don't worry. You can drive there in 20 minutes, don't you?

Richard： Yes, but I sent my car to a mechanic place for service.

David： What's wrong with it?

Richard： Nothing serious. Just an annual service and get the brake pads replaced.

David： How long have you been driving this car?

Richard： About 6 months. Recently the brake didn't respond very well. So I think it might need a new brake pad.

David： Oh, I see. I'm going downtown for shopping with my girlfriend. I can give you a lift if you like.

Richard： Are you sure it's OK? I don't want to disturb you guys.

David： Yep, I am positive.

Richard: That would be great.

David: Where are you meeting your client?

Richard: In a cafe on the east end of Long Street. But if you can drop me somewhere close to the big department store, that'll be fine.

David: I'll take you there. Long Street isn't far out of my way anyway.

Richard: What a pal!

David: I'll get the car from the parking lot right now.

Richard: Good. I'll meet you at the gate in ten minutes.

David: OK.

Richard: (*On the way.*) I know we are in a hurry, but you should always drive within the speed limit, shouldn't you? I just saw a speed limit sign. It says 60 kilometers per hour!

David: Don't be a back seat driver. I've been over this road a million times. I know it like the back of my hand and can even drive with my eyes closed.

Richard: Last year when we were driving to a construction site in Jinshan, you drove so fast that I was almost scared to death and a week later you got a speeding ticket. Remember?

David: Sure I remember. I didn't expect they had a camera installed on that part of the road.

Richard: You are not driving for those cameras, are you?

David: I guess so.

Richard: Wow! Did you see that car accident on the side of the road? That's the third one we've passed today!

David: OK, OK. Don't be a nag. I'll slow down.

Dialogue B   To the Railway Station

Richard is looking at a dozen of bus route signs at a bus stop and he is puzzled and does not know which bus can take him to the railway station.

Richard: Excuse me, ma'am. I'm trying to get to the Shanghai Railway Station. Which bus should I take?

Woman: Let me see. You're on the wrong street. You have to walk two more blocks to Yan'an Road. At the corner, you will see a No. 936 bus stop. It will take you to the railway station.

Richard: Thank you very much. I really appreciate your help.

Man: Young man, I couldn't help but overheard your conversation with the lady who just gave you direction.

Richard: Yes?

Man: I think she must be confused. The direction she gave you is wrong. If you follow her, you'll end up at the zoo!

Richard: Really? What should I do, then?

Man: You can't get there directly with a No. 936 Bus. You'll have to change buses. First, you take the No. 936 Bus. Get off at Shi Men Road stop, and then take the No. 104 Bus, which terminates at the railway station.

Richard: How long will it take to get there?

Man: At least one and a half hours.

Richard: It seems I have to take a taxi.

Man: That won't help much. You know, West Street is a very busy commercial street. Cars always get jammed there at rush hour. Besides, it's almost impossible to find a taxi available during rush hour.

Richard: My God! My train leaves in an hour. I'll miss it.

Man: Why don't you go there by subway? It'll take you there in about half an hour.

Richard: Is the subway station far from here?

Man: Not at all! It's just on the opposite side of the road.

Richard: How often are the trains?

Man: Every five to six minutes.

Richard: That's great! Thank you very much. You're a life saver.

Man: That's my pleasure.

(At the subway station Richard walks to a customer service agent for help.)

Richard: Excuse me, how do I get to the Shanghai Railway Station?

Agent: Take Line 2 to the People's Square, then change to Line 1 and get off at the Railway Station. Make sure you're on the right platform.

Richard: Which platform is it on?

Agent: Platform 1. Go down the stairs over there. It's on your right hand side.

Richard: Thanks a lot.

Agent: You're welcome.

Dialogue C   At Shanghai Expo

After the security checking at Expo Gate Two, Ying and Richard don't know which way they should take. Ying sees a volunteer at the staircase of the elevated path and walks over to ask her.

Ying: Excuse me. We'd like to take a tour at United States Pavilion first and then China Pavilion on the way back. Could you tell me where the United States

Pavilion is?

Volunteer: Sure. We are now at Zone D. The Pavilion is in Zone C, which is located on the other side of the river.

Richard: Are you suggesting that we must cross the Huangpu River? It would be a bit far, I'm afraid.

Volunteer: Yes, if you want to visit United States Pavilion first.

Ying: Don't worry. There are some buses in the Expo Park, I know.

Volunteer: Yes, there are four bus lines within the Expo Park, all free of charge. There are also five sightseeing lines, but you'll be charged 10 RMB each person.

Ying: How about we take a ferry ride?

Volunteer: Of course you can take ferry. There are three ferry piers in Puxi.

Ying: How can we get there?

Volunteer: Well, I will suggest you to take Expo Cross-river Bus Line. It's fast and convenient. It starts from Enterprise Pavilion and stops at Asia Pavilion, China Pavilion and Theme Pavilion, then terminates at Central and South American Pavilion, which is close to the United States Pavilion.

Richard: Sounds great! Shall we take this ... en ... Expo River Bus, Ying?

Volunteer: Expo Cross-river Bus Line, which is also named as Bus Line 1.

Richard: Yes, Expo Cross-river Bus Line. Thank you.

Ying: I prefer taking the ferry, if you don't mind, Richard.

Richard: No, not a bit. (*Turn to the volunteer.*) Any bus line from here to the ferry pier?

Volunteer: (*Points on the map.*) There is a bus stop over there. Step onto the elevated path and walk about 100 meters. You will see the bus stop on your left side on the ground. Please take Puxi Sightseeing Line, which stops at L3 Ferry Terminal. It is a pay minibus, 10 RMB per head.

Ying: But shall we walk to the ferry pier, Richard? It's not far from here, believe me.

Richard: Miss, I need your suggestion, please.

Volunteer: Not far at all. About 10 minutes walk. Walk along the elevated path till the end and you can see the pier on your right side.

Richard: Thank you very much. Oh, excuse me. I've got one more question. Which bus can we take after getting off the boat?

Volunteer: Well, there is no bus stop at Pudong ferry piers. But if you walk about 5 minutes and there is a bus stop near the Baosteel Stage on Expo Avenue. Get off at Houtan Entrance & Exit. The United States Pavilion is south to the Africa Joint Pavilion. Just two blocks away.

Richard: Thank you very much.

Volunteer: Here is the map. You may also need it.

Richard:	Thank you. We appreciate your help.
Volunteer:	You are welcome.
Richard:	Bye.
Volunteer:	Have a nice day and enjoy yourself.
Richard:	(*After walking away about two minutes.*) We are lucky. We might have met the most excellent volunteer.
Ying:	Yes, she is. They've got 79 thousand volunteers. She must be one of the best.

Dialogue D   High-speed Era

Richard is going to attend a meeting in Hangzhou tomorrow. He is packing his luggage now. Henry and Sophia are watching TV.

Sophia:	Where are you going this time, Richard?
Richard:	Just a routine business trip to Hangzhou.
Sophia:	Are you going there with David?
Richard:	No, not this time. He'll stay here and look after another project.
Sophia:	Hopefully not. You do know he drives too fast, don't you?
Richard:	I know, Mom. I told him that. And he said he will be driving more carefully.
Sophia:	Then how do you get there?
Richard:	By train, I guess.
Sophia:	By train? You don't know that the Spring Festival is the peak traveling season in China, do you? This year about 230 million passengers are expected to travel back home by train for family reunions. It's hard to get a ticket.
Richard:	Don't worry. I'll take an intercity high-speed train to Hangzhou. The tickets are available all the time.
Henry:	There is no denying that high-speed trains have made traveling more convenient and shortened travel time. But comparing with other means of transportation like ordinary trains, buses and planes, high-speed railway trains attract fewer passengers, due to their super expensive fares. Tickets are beyond the reach of the majority of migrant workers and students.
Richard:	That's true. Take a ticket to Hangzhou for example. A high-speed train ticket is 82 *yuan*, while the ordinary train ticket only costs you 29 *yuan*.
Sophia:	Oh, my God, it's almost three times dearer. That makes a huge difference!
Richard:	Exactly!
Henry:	Even an official of the Ministry of Railways admits that until now, high-

speed railways have not shown any signs of relieving the pressure on the transport network during the Spring Festival travel season.

Richard： The transport problem during the Spring Festival travel season highlights a contradiction：The world's largest movement of people needs more transport facilities，but the need is only limited to a couple of months in a year. This dilemma is and will keep many people from enjoying easy and comfortable travel during the Spring Festival for years.

Henry： Well，the government has made great efforts to improve the transport infrastructure. It is said that China is planning to build a maglev railway between Shanghai and Hangzhou. According to the proposed design，the speed is 450 km/h and it takes only 27 minutes from Shanghai to Hangzhou. Obviously China is entering into a high-speed transportation era.

Richard： But I reckon the ticket price will go sky high，far beyond ordinary people's affordability. The emphasis on high-speed railways may not meet people's needs. Greater efforts should be made to build more conventional speed railways，which ordinary people can afford. Anyway，people need more travel choices.

Sophia： That's the point.

Notes

1.	token	(乘车用)代金硬币
2.	What's the time by your watch?	你的表几点了?
3.	I'm gonna	口语中常用 be gonna 代替 be going to
4.	mechanic place	修车店
5.	annual service	汽车年度保养
6.	brake pad	刹车片
7.	give you a lift	让你搭个便车
8.	What a pal!	真不愧是好朋友!
9.	the parking lot	停车场
10.	Don't be a back seat driver.	别坐在后排指挥。
11.	almost scared to death	吓得半死
12.	speeding ticket	超速罚单
13.	Don't be a nag.	别唠叨啦!
14.	get jammed	塞车;被卡住
15.	at rush hour	上下班高峰时段
16.	customer service agent	客户服务助理

17. volunteer   志愿者
18. elevated path   高架步行道
19. United States Pavilion   美国馆
20. sightseeing lines   观光游览公交线路
21. ferry pier   轮渡码头
22. Puxi   此处指的是 2010 上海世博浦西展区
23. Theme Pavilion   主题馆
24. per head   每人
25. Baosteel Stage   宝钢大舞台
26. Houtan Entrance & Exit   后滩出入口
27. beyond the reach   超出……能力之外
28. migrant workers   农民工
29. almost three times dearer   差不多贵了三倍
30. Ministry of Railways   铁道部
31. relieve the pressure   缓解压力
32. highlight a contradiction   使矛盾突出
33. Maglev   磁悬浮
34. end up   以……为终点

 ## Functional Expressions

Stating What You Want

1. A salad and a piece of bread would go down well.
2. I could do with some exercise.
3. I feel like a drink now.
4. I need to know all the facts.
5. I think I'll have a cup of coffee.
6. I want to have a bite of it.
7. I wouldn't mind a ride in that car.
8. I'd give anything to have a go on that merry-go-round.
9. I'd like to have a look at it.
10. I'm dying for a look at Summer Palace.
11. It'd be nice to have some rest.
12. What I need is a good sleep.
13. What she wants is a hot bath.

Quarreling with Somebody

1. Are you trying to make a fool of me?
2. Cut it out! I've had enough of that.
3. Drop it! It's enough.
4. How can you do that to me?
5. How dare you!
6. I think you've gone much too far.
7. It's none of your business.
8. I've just come to the end of my patience.
9. She's just about had enough.
10. Stop it! I can't stand it any more!
11. That's really too much!
12. Well, of all the nerve!
13. What do you think you are?
14. What's that got to do with it?
15. Who gives you the right to behave like that?
16. You got a nerve to do that to me.
17. You have absolutely no right to do that.
18. You're caring your jokes too far!
19. You're getting on my nerves.

Expressing Optimistic Views

1. Everything will be fine.
2. It'll all turn out fine.
3. It's all going to be OK.
4. That'll be great, I'm sure.
5. The plan can't go wrong.
6. The visiting team is bound to win.
7. Things'll work out all right.
8. You wait and see. Everything will turn out all right.

 Communicative Task

The Best Tour Proposal

Types of Task: group, class.

Functions Practiced: asking for directions, stating what you want to do, asking for advice, expressing optimistic views.

Pre-task

1. Read the following map. It shows main streets, highways, and freeways in Delano, California, USA.

2. When you are reading the map keep the following questions in your mind:

> Why were the streets so named?
> Is it convenient for a stranger to locate a specific place or street in the city?
> Do you like this particular way of naming a street? Why?
> What about the street names in your hometown? Were they named in a different way or a similar way?

3. To best complete the task reorganize your group into group of three.

4. Discuss with your group members about the way of naming a street in this city. Use some questions on step 2 to start your inquiry.

5. Find all the abbreviations used on the map and try to guess the meanings of these abbreviations. Discuss them in your group or look them up in your dictionary, if necessary.

6. Work individually over one of the following subtasks:

1) Student A draws a hospital, two post offices and two cinemas on the map;

2) Student B adds two shopping centers, two parks and two sports centers to the map;

3) Student C develops six bus routes for the city and labels all the stops on the map.

7. After all of you have completed the subtasks, release only part of your information to others in the group. For example,

1) Student A informs the others only of the names of the hospital, post offices and cinemas;

2) Student B lets the others know only the rough locations for shopping centers, parks and sports centers;

3) Student C tells only the terminals for each bus route, not every stop along a bus route.

8. Suppose Student A lives on Spring Ave., Student B Clinton St. and Student C Browning Rd. near York St.

9. Each of you has something to do in the city and wants the others to go with him. For example:

Student A needs to see a friend in a hospital;

Student B wants to pick up a parcel at a post office;

Student C would like to go skating at a sports center.

10. Unfortunately, all of you have only incomplete information and what's more, taxi drivers are on strike at the moment.

11. Now sit back to back in your group and begin to phone each other to tell the other what you want to do and ask the right person for the necessary information to complete your adventure in a foreign city.

The Map of Delano, CA, USA

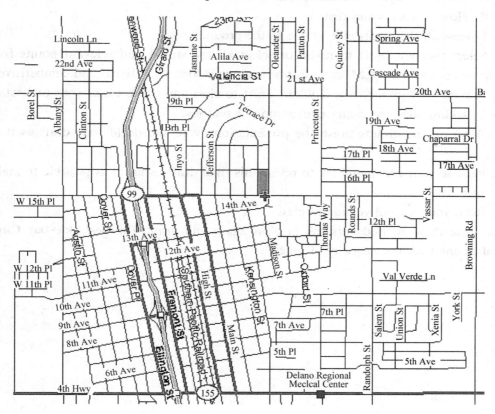

Task Procedure

1. Now in your regular group the group leader reads the following Announcement to the group and it is the group leader's responsibility to make sure all members understand it. Read loud enough for the rest of the group.

Announcement

The city authorities have recognized the positive effect of tourism on the social and economical development for our city and decided to hold a seminar on developing several one-day city tour programs in the city hall next week. Our school has decided to hold a contest to select the best one-day city tour program and the winner of the contest would deliver the proposal at the seminar on behalf of our school.

2. Each one in the group now starts to write a draft for **The Best Tour Proposal**.
3. Your proposal should at least cover:
   1) Who — prospective tourists
   2) What — theme of the tour

3）Where — sights and attractions

4）How — routes and costs

4. Discuss all the drafts one by one in the group.

5. Select the best draft to revise or select all the strong and relevant points from all drafts to make a new one. Make sure this new one is logical，rational and competitive.

6. Present your group's one-day tour draft to class and try to make your presentation a success by adding some necessary explanation or reasons.

7. After all the groups finish the presentation，vote and decide one draft as the final draft.

8. Back to your group and try to revise this final draft as much as possible to make it a perfect one.

9. Read your revised version to class.

10. Vote these revised versions in class again and grant **The Best One-Day City Tour Proposal** to one with the majority of votes.

Unit Thirteen

Seeing the Doctor

 Warm Up

1. Say out Loud and Fast

1) His diarrhea is caused by colibacillus.
2) Anna King thinks local anesthesia will do for the operation.
3) They'll operate on you for appendicitis.
4) Johnson visits his patients at their homes at regular intervals.
5) The child is running a high fever. We must send for a doctor at once.
6) The doctor prescribed a new medicine for the pain in my joints.
7) Each year about 200 new cases of HIV infection are diagnosed.
8) I have chronic asthma which is more than moderate in severity.
9) Some hepatitis B victims can have further problems.
10) Bird flu is a contagious disease caused by TYPE A flu virus.

2. Culture Tip

The National Health Service in the United Kingdom is based on the idea that medical care should be available to everyone, at little or no cost. Health services are available largely free of charge to every resident in Britain.

In the United States most people purchase private health insurance to protect themselves against financial hardships that can result from expenses for physicians, hospital care, and other medical treatments, since free medical care is minimal. Insurance is merely a means by which they pool money to guard against the sudden economic consequences of sickness or injury.

The development of medical knowledge in the West has brought about certain rules of behavior in the sickroom that are sometimes different from ways of acting in the Orient. "Doctor's orders" are obeyed almost as strictly as civil laws. Therefore, if you have a friend who is under the doctor's care, it is right to find out what rules the doctor has laid down as to visits, food or other requirements before you go to see him.

 **Dialogues**

Dialogue A   Insomnia

Isabel has been so worried about her exams these days that she couldn't get to sleep at night. She goes to the clinic in the school.

Doctor: What can I do for you, Miss?

Isabel: It's very bad, doctor. I keep feeling dizzy, and I've got a headache. It's so painful that I can hardly fall asleep. Even worse, I have no appetite for anything.

Doctor: How long has it been going on?

Isabel: It came on at the beginning of this week.

Doctor: So it's almost a week. Do you stay up late?

Isabel: Yes, I've been preparing for my finals. Last night, I worked on my paper for a whole night and slept about three hours. When I got up this morning, I felt dizzy and fell. So I had to come to you.

Doctor: I see. I'm afraid you're in a run-down condition. It generally happens to students at the end of a semester. Physically, you work too hard; psychologically, you're too nervous. As a result, you're exhausted.

Isabel: What shall I do? Do I need to take any pills?

Doctor: No, you needn't. Nothing serious at all. Just relax and do some exercises. Don't study for too long at any one time. And have a sound sleep before an exam, otherwise you may ruin it.

Isabel: But doctor, I've had insomnia these days. Any good ideas?

Doctor: It's good for you to do some exercise at intervals. Or have a glass of milk before going to bed.

Isabel: Is music helpful?

Doctor: It depends. Don't tell me you like listening to rock music at night.

Isabel: Of course not. But it's said classical music has the same effect as a lullaby.

Doctor: You're right. But it is important to keep a good habit to sleep before midnight, as the old saying goes, "One hour's sleep before midnight is worth two after." Anyhow, good luck in your exams.

Isabel: Thank you very much.

Doctor: My pleasure.

Dialogue B   A Medical Check

Mrs. Sophia White has felt unwell for a couple of days and goes to see her doctor this afternoon.

Doctor: What's troubling you?

Sophia: I'm not very well. I've got a sore throat and a cough. When I cough, it's painful in the chest.

Doctor: What is your body temperature?

Sophia: I've been running a high temperature since yesterday. It is 38.5, the nurse told me just now.

Doctor: How long have you felt this way?

Sophia: Two days.

Doctor: Why didn't you come to the hospital yesterday?

Sophia: I thought it was the flu. When I was down with flu, I used to take some pills, and it would be over in a couple of days. But this time it doesn't work.

Doctor: Considering your own description of the symptom, I don't think it's flu. I suggest you have a blood test and an X-ray scan for your chest.

Sophia: What's wrong with me?

Doctor: I cannot tell until I see the report.

          (*After blood and X-ray tests.*)

Sophia: How's the result, doctor? Do I have tuberculosis?

Doctor: The report says your blood is normal, yet there is a light infection in your right lung.

Sophia: Is it serious?

Doctor: Nothing serious if you take medicine on time. But you must stay in bed for a week or two. And you'd stay at home until you are completely recovered.

Sophia: I see. Can I have the prescription now?

Doctor: Here it is. This medicine can get rid of the infection in your lung. You take two tablets every six hours. Drink a lot of hot water, and don't have any heavy food.

Sophia: Can I have a bath?

Doctor：   Yes，you can. Keep warm, and be careful not to catch a cold, otherwise it'll make things worse. By the way, if you feel dizzy after you take the pills, please let me know.

Sophia：   I will.

Dialogue C   At the Dentist's

Isabel has been suffering from a toothache for several days and she wants to make an appointment with the dentist. She rings the dentist's office. Julie, receptionist of Dr. Brown Dental Surgery, picks up the phone.

Julie：   Dr. Brown Dental Surgery. This is Julie. Can I help you?

Isabel：   Hi, this is Isabel. I wonder if Dr. Brown could fit me in early tomorrow morning.

Julie：   Sorry, Dr. Brown is not available tomorrow morning.

Isabel：   Would 1:00 be convenient?

Julie：   That's not good, either. He won't be back from his lunch break until 1:30.

Isabel：   I see. What time is he free in the afternoon?

Julie：   Just a second, let me check ... You're lucky. There's a cancellation at 2:30. You may come then.

Isabel：   Really? That's great. Thank you very much.

Julie：   May I know your full name, please?

Isabel：   Isabel, Isabel White.

Julie：   What's your contact number, please?

Isabel：   It's 462 - 1753.

Julie：   See you tomorrow, Isabel.

Isabel：   See you.

(*At the dentist's.*)

Dr. Brown：   How long have you been like this?

Isabel：   It's been three or four days now. I can't eat anything. Anything, hot or cold, sweet or sour, hurts me.

Dr. Brown：   Have you had this before?

Isabel：   Yes, it's been troubling me for several times.

Dr. Brown：   Now please open your mouth as wide as you can ... well, I think you'd better take an X-ray.

Isabel：   Can't you see anything?

Dr. Brown：   You've got an abscess and an impacted molar. It's too late. I don't think we can save the tooth.

Isabel:	How bad is it?
Dr. Brown:	It's quite serious. You need a surgical extraction of the impacted molar.
Isabel:	Will it hurt?
Dr. Brown:	Not during the operation. But it'll hurt you afterwards.
Isabel:	That's too bad.
Dr. Brown:	Don't worry. I'll give you some pills. They can relieve the pain.
Isabel:	That's great. By the way, how soon can I eat?
Dr. Brown:	Not for two days. You need a "soft food" diet today and tomorrow.
Isabel:	Something easy to chew and swallow?
Dr. Brown:	Right. Yogurt, scrambled eggs, and white bread for breakfast. Tomato soup, tuna salad, mashed potatoes, cheese ravioli, and quiche for lunch and dinner, for example.
Isabel:	What about rice and beans?
Dr. Brown:	Not today, at least. Creamy risotto or tiny couscous can be scratchy and hard to swallow. Stick to potatoes or pasta instead. Individual black beans aren't hard to chew, but parts of their skin tend to get stuck in teeth.
Isabel:	Can I have chicken breast?
Dr. Brown:	Even the softest chicken breast is a challenge when it's hard to chew and swallow, but chicken salad is a good option, if you like chicken. Now please follow me to the X-ray room.

Dialogue D   Feeling Funny

Richard feels funny today. David Smith, his colleague, suspects there must be something wrong with Richard.

David:	Morning, Richard. Oh, you don't look well today, pal.
Richard:	I've got a headache and feel a bit shivery.
David:	You might have a fever. You need to see a doctor.
Richard:	I think I'd better. Could you call a cab for me? And if there're any calls for me, please ask them to leave a message and I'll call them back when I get back to the office.
David:	Sure. Let me take you to the cab.
	(*At the doctor's.*)
Doctor:	Well, what can I do for you?
Richard:	I've got a sore throat and I seem to have a fever now and then. I feel so weak that I can't support myself.

Doctor:	Any vomiting?
Richard:	No. But I don't feel like eating.
Doctor:	Let me take your temperature. Hmm . . . you're running a fever.
Richard:	Anything serious?
Doctor:	No, nothing at all. But a couple of shots will be of some help.
Richard:	Shots make me nervous.
Doctor:	You're not alone. Lots of people dread them because they have a very real fear of needles.
Richard:	I'm one of them, Doc. Sometimes people even feel lightheaded or faint after getting a shot.
Doctor:	There are some ways to help you relax.
Richard:	I need your professional advice, Doc.
Doctor:	For example, distract yourself while you're waiting, taking slow, deep breaths and focusing intently on something in the room. Deep breathing can help people relax and concentrating on something other than the shot can take your mind off it. Research even shows that coughing as the needle goes in can help some people feel less pain. Of course, try to relax your arm. If you're tense, especially if you tense up the area where you're getting the shot, it can make a shot hurt more. If you feel funny afterwards, sit down and rest for 15 minutes.
Richard:	Thank you very much, Doc.
Doctor:	My pleasure. Now here are some pills. Take one every four hours, and . . .
Richard:	Is that aspirin? I'm allergic to aspirin.
Doctor:	No, it isn't. It is made of extractions from Chinese traditional herbs. It's mild but effective.
Richard:	All right.
Doctor:	You need a good rest and take some days off work as well.
Richard:	How long do I need to stay in bed? You know, I plan to go on a business trip soon.
Doctor:	Two days, I'm afraid. I hope you'll be sufficiently recovered before going to work. Young man, work is only one part of life.
Richard:	I know, there is more in life than work. But I've got so much to do every day. Thank you for your advice.
Doctor:	Take care of yourself then. If you don't feel any better, come back to me immediately.
Richard:	Thanks a lot.

Notes

1.	insomnia	失眠
2.	I have no appetite for anything.	我没胃口。
3.	stay up late	熬夜
4.	finals	期末考试
5.	run-down	虚弱，疲乏；走下坡路
6.	semester	学期
7.	As a result, you're exhausted.	结果累垮了。
8.	do some exercise at intervals	（学习之间）运动一下
9.	It depends.	这要区别对待。
10.	lullaby	催眠曲
11.	I thought it was the flu.	我本以为得了流感。
12.	tuberculosis	肺结核
13.	a light infection	轻度感染
14.	heavy food	油腻的食物
15.	feel funny	感觉不舒服
16.	fit me in early tomorrow morning	把我安排在明天一早
17.	abscess	脓肿
18.	molar	臼齿
19.	a surgical extraction	拔牙手术
20.	relieve the pain	镇痛
21.	a "soft food" diet	易消化的膳食搭配
22.	chew and swallow	咀嚼与吞咽
23.	yogurt	酸奶
24.	scrambled egg	炒蛋
25.	tuna salad	金枪鱼色拉
26.	cheese ravioli	意大利干酪饺子
27.	quiche	法式咸派；乳蛋饼
28.	risotto	意大利烩饭
29.	couscous	古斯古斯米（原产于中东、北非）
30.	scratchy	粗糙的
31.	pasta	面制食品
32.	get stuck in teeth	塞牙
33.	I can't support myself.	我连站都站不起来。
34.	Any vomiting?	呕吐吗？
35.	Doc(Doctor)	医生

36. lightheaded	头昏眼花
37. allergic	过敏
38. extractions from Chinese traditional herbs	中草药提炼物
39. shot	肌肉注射

 Functional Expressions

Feeling Disappointed

1. His decision's a great pity.

2. I don't think much of the operation Simon had yesterday.

3. I was rather disappointed at not getting the tickets.

4. I'd expected it to be much better.

5. I'm sorry to hear about his failure in the examinations.

6. It wasn't as good as I'd expected.

7. It's a real pity.

8. It's disappointing!

9. Oh dear, I was hoping for a chance to enjoy the opera.

10. Oh my, the doctor says I'd be confined to bed for another week.

11. That's a real letdown.

12. That's a shame.

13. That's very disappointing, I must say.

14. The performance could have been better.

15. The play wasn't as good as I thought it would be.

16. Their suggestion wasn't up to much.

17. What a pity!

18. What a shame!

Expressing Worries or Fears

1. I do hope Bob will get well soon.

2. I was frightened to death when the doctor told me the truth.

3. I was scared out of my wits, giving my first performance.

4. I'm afraid of injections in the school clinic.

5. I'm afraid to tell him that he has a tumor in his kidney.

6. I'm really terrified to witness the slaughter.

7. I'm all wound up about her health.

8. You frightened me out of my mind, saying you wanted to kill yourself.

9. You scared me out of my mind coming up behind me suddenly like that.

Expressing Dismal Feeling

1. How could he do such a thing to me?
2. I can't take much more of this.
3. I don't feel at all happy.
4. I wish I hadn't come here.
5. It's just been one of those days.
6. I've got a lot on my mind.
7. Just think, all that work for nothing.
8. Oh, I don't know. I'm just a bit depressed, that's all.
9. Oh, no! How could this happen to me!
10. Really. I'm just feeling a bit low, that's all.
11. Things're getting me down a bit.
12. To think that I went to all that trouble for nothing.
13. What damned luck!

Communicative Task

A Wrong Case of Dental Extraction

Types of Task: pair, group, class.

Functions Practiced: asking for personal health information, expressing worry or fear, complaining, apologizing.

Pre-task

1. Your school clinic decides to carry out a survey of personal health for the new students. The requirements for the survey are given below. You and your pair are both asked by your school clinic to collect the health information from each other so that they can keep a record for emergency.

2. Read silently the following survey table by yourself. Make sure you know the meaning and pronunciation of some medical terms. Use your dictionary if necessary.

3. If you decide you will be the first one to start this survey, tell your pair to close the textbook while you are doing an oral survey based on the following requirements.

4. Ask your pair for her/his personal medical history apart from the above information. For example, what disease did he or she get in the childhood? What accident did his/her relatives happen to be involved? What sequela has ever affected them?

5. You need to write down as much as possible and as accurate as you can your pair's

answers to all the questions listed in the table.

6. Reverse the roles with your pair.

7. Now join your regular group, select one item in the table concerning your health problems or your relatives' problems and express your worries or fears to your group members. For example, you bruise easily, your relatives suffer from migraine headaches, or you are going to donate blood next week. They may offer you some advice to remove your worries.

Personal Health Information

Name:　　　　　　Sex:　　　　　　　Height:　　　　　Weight: Date of Birth:　　Blood Type:　　Allergic to: 1.　　　2.	
Do you go for regular medical check-ups?	
Have you ever sprained your ankle?	
Do you bruise easily?	
Do you suffer from migraine headaches?	
Have you ever broken a bone?	
When was the last time you went to a doctor? A dentist?	
How often do you get sick in one year?	
How many hours of sleep do you usually get?	
Do you have false teeth?	
Have you ever been hospitalized?	
Have you ever taken a sleeping pill to get to sleep?	
Do you suffer from backaches?	
Do you go to the dentist's twice a year?	
Do you watch your weight?	
Do you take vitamins or mineral supplements?	
Have you ever had stitches?	
Have you ever been to an acupuncturist?	
Do you take medicine when you are sick?	
Have you ever donated blood?	
If you smoke, how old were you when you started smoking?	
What are some ways you know that you can personally keep yourself healthy?	

Task Procedure

1. Now read the Task Direction for the pictures posted below.

Task Direction

Jack's toothache is so terrible that he cannot speak a word clearly. To make it worse he just came from Egypt and cannot write in English or Chinese. Therefore, he draws four pictures to tell you his ill fortune in a clinic next to your school.

2. Look carefully at the pictures and ponder over what happens to Jack.

3. Try your best to figure out the cause of Jack's bad luck in the clinic and write down what you believe might have happened to Jack under each relevant picture.

4. Tell your group members what you think might have happened to Jack.

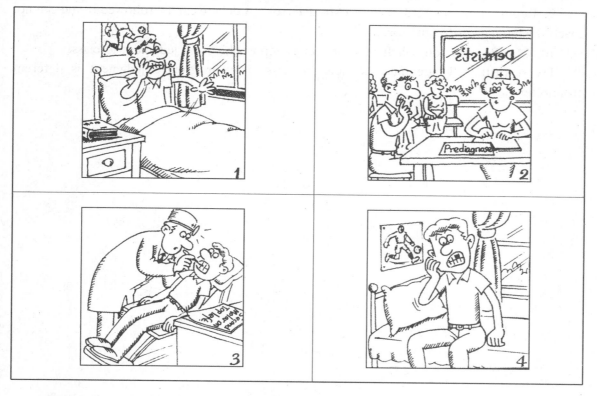

5. After making sure what has happened to Jack, work with your group members to write a complaint letter for Jack to your school authorities and demand justice for Jack.

6. Your school administration is very concerned about Jack's case. Mr. Pearson (acted by one student from other group), the coordinator from the school is now with your group and wants you to act out the incident from the very beginning in detail so that he can see what is wrong and who is responsible for the case. Now assign the roles among your members and invite one of your fellow students as Mr. Pearson.

7. Dramatize this play in your group. Roles are listed in the cast.

Cast

1) Mr. Pearson .... school coordinator
2) Jack .... student
3) Dr. Henry Slipshod .... dentist in the clinic
4) Ms. Jane Kareless .... intern nurse in the clinic
5) Narrator（introducing background information for the role-play）

8. At the end of your role-play，an apologizing meeting should also be included. You and your group members must make a judgment：who should be responsible for the case，and who should apologize based on your interpretation of the pictures.

9. Report your group's decision to Mr. Pearson. A debate can be followed if you can not reach the agreement for the case.

10. Mr. Pearson，on behalf of your group，reports his final judgment to class.

11. A further debate must be held in class，if your group's judgment is deferent from others'.

Unit Fourteen

Sports and Exercises

 Warm Up

1. Say out Loud and Fast

1) Playing sports helps to build confidence when you see your skills improving and your goals becoming reality.

2) If you're great at volleyball but would rather play soccer because you think it's more fun, then just do it!

3) On particularly nice days, I kick around the soccer ball, toss around the baseball, or go on long runs.

4) Pilates is a body conditioning routine that seeks to build flexibility, strength, endurance, and coordination without adding muscle bulk.

5) They're facing a dilemma a lot of teens face — which sports to play and which sports to give up.

6) Sprained ankles are the most common basketball injuries, but broken fingers, bruises, bloody or broken noses, and poked eyes are all too common as well.

7) When playing outdoors, abrasions on the palms and fingers are always a risk.

8) Helmets are important for sports such as hockey, baseball, softball, biking, skateboarding, inline skating, skiing, and snowboarding — to name just a few.

9) Getting the right amount of exercise can rev up your energy levels and even help improve your mood.

10) After playing a sport or a game, congratulate the other players on their playing ability and let them know that you enjoyed playing with them.

2. Culture Tip

There are two species of sports that Americans are passionate about. One is the varsity sports events that are televised and students and alumni ardently support their college team in the stadium and before television. The other is the professional leagues, and each team in such a league represents a city, a state or an area. The most well-known professional league is NBA, the National Basketball Association.

However, most Americans also regard baseball, softball and American football as their national sports. But American football, rather like rugby in Britain and played between two teams of 11 players using an oval ball that can be handled or kicked, is different from the football played in the United Kingdom. During the past ten years or so, ice hockey has gradually gained its popularity in the States yet Canada still dominates that sport as their national sport.

The United Kingdom and the Commonwealth in general share such sports as rugby and cricket. These sports are also played in Hong Kong and rugby is played in France, too.

Despite the popularity of sports in the US and other countries, obesity is still a problem. Westerners in general tend to be sensitive about being fat and so it is impolite to refer to overweight people as "fat" or even draw attention to it.

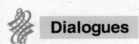

Dialogues

Dialogue A   Richard the Rotund (I)

Richard White talks with his personal trainer, Mr. Adam Scott, in the gym.

Adam: Hi, Richard! Long time no see.

Richard: Yeah, I've been out on a business trip for three weeks, and then was dragged into this new company expansion project until now. How about you?

Adam: Same as usual, tutoring here four to five days a week, preparing for the body building contest which will hold in the middle of November, working in a bar for a few nights during the week if I'm not busy with other stuff.

Richard: Oh, I saw you got some new equipment here.

Adam: Yes, we have imported quite a lot of latest equipments from the US a couple of months ago.

Richard: Ah, what does that machine over there for?

Adam: Well, it is a Roman Chair. I developed a back extension exercise based on its features to target the erector spinae, gluteals and hamstrings.

Richard: May I have a try?

Adam: Sure. Position your thighs on the pads of the Roman chair. Make sure your hips are free to flex. Put your feet flat on the foot supports, your spine neutral and your elbows pointing out. Then, flex at your hips and drop your upper body towards the floor and keep you back flat.

Richard: What's the next?

Adam: Keep your movement slow and controlled. Stop bending when you feel your hamstrings restricts further movement. The third step is to return to the start position.

Richard: And then repeat again?

Adam: Yes, but contract your hamstrings, glutes, and spinal erectors. Remember: do not extend beyond the start position to avoid hurting your back.

Richard: A lot of exercises around the hip joints.

Adam: Yep, that's the purpose. Back to business. What can I do for you this time?

Richard: Well, as you know, I haven't exercised for three weeks and accumulated some fat around waist and I want to get my muscles back.

Adam: Like the old saying "Use it or lose it". Since you haven't trained for a long time, too much strenuous exercise may hurt you. You'd better begin with some warm-up routines.

Richard: I see. What exercise do you recommend me to do?

Adam: Follow me.

Richard: OK. I'm ready.

Adam: This is called Hip Circle. Stand upright with your hands on your hips, your legs straight, and your feet shoulder-width or slightly more apart. Start to rotate your hips slowly in a clockwise direction.

Richard: Like this?

Adam: No, don't arch your lower back and look straight ahead.

Richard: I got it.

Adam: Good. Repeat it ten times. Then reverse your direction, rotating anticlockwise.

Richard: I feel good.

Adam: Now, Torso Rotation. Raise your elbows to each side and keep your forearms inline with your shoulders. Rotate your upper body with a smooth motion to your right. Rotate back through the start position and continue to your left, keeping your elbows up. Return to the start position.

Richard: I feel dizzy now.

Adam: Richard, slow down. You're too fast. You need to rotate smoothly and keep your head up and level throughout.

Richard: OK. Now it's better.

Adam: Stand upright，with your arms by your sides and close to your body. Keep your shoulders relaxed. Flex your upper body sideways，sliding your left hand down your leg as far as it will go.

Richard: Am I correct?

Adam: Sort of. Try don't lean forwards or back and don't "bounce" at the end of the movement.

Richard: OK?

Adam: Now it's better. Repeat for your right hand side. Keep in mind，move only your upper body and from side to side. Do this ten times.

Richard: One. Two. Three ... Eight. Nine. Ten.

(*To be continued.*)

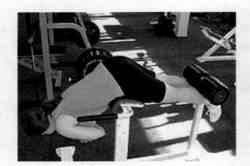

A *back extension*

Dialogue B　Richard the Rotund (Ⅱ)

Previously，Adam shows Richard some warm-up movements. Now the real exercise begins.

Adam: Good. We move back to the Roman Chair to do some stretch.

Richard: The same as we did before?

Adam: No. I'll let you bend sideways to exercise your external obliques and internal obliques.

Richard: What do I do?

Adam: Lie sideways on the Roman Chair. Adjust it so that your upper body can turn comfortably at your hips towards the floor. Hold your hands at head level.

Richard: Tell me this won't be hard.

Adam: No, it won't. Just relax. Now lean slowly sideways towards the floor as far as is comfortable. Breathe in on the descent.

Richard: Do I need to hold it?

Adam: Yes, if you can. But don't hold for too long, it can tear your muscle.

Richard: Yes, sir.

Adam: Now gently raise your body back to the start position. Breathe out on the upward movement. Do this eight times on one side then repeat on the other side.

Richard: (*After he finishes the movements.*) Wow, after this I do feel the tension in my external obliques.

Adam: You bet. Now we move to the bench and do a few V-leg Raises.

Richard: OK.

Adam: Richard, sit on the bench, please, supporting yourself by gripping the pad behind you. Lift your legs together, keeping your toes pointed.

Richard: Balancing my body on the edge of the bench is quite challenging.

Adam: You can do it, Richard, trust me. Now keep your feet and knees together, bend your knees and bring them towards your chest. Pull your torso forwards a little for balance. Bring your knees as close to your body as possible. And hold.

Richard: You know, I always trust you. But my abdomen feels sore.

Adam: That's right. This exercise provides a powerful workout for your abdominal muscles. You can put a weight on your ankles to boost the intensity. Now extending your hips and knees to return to the start position.

Richard: How many times do I need to repeat?

Adam: As many as you can. But considering you haven't trained for a long time, I think four times is a good start.

Richard: OK. I'll try my best.

Adam: One. Two. Three. Four. Well done. Now you can relax. Jump on the treadmill, select cool down function and walk for 5 minutes. This allows your heart rate to go below 100 bpm and will prevent muscle cramps or something worse.

Richard: I'll remember that.

Adam: Great. Then come back tomorrow we'll do more sessions.

Dialogue C   Yoga Class

It's 11:00 Saturday morning. Sophia comes back home in white loose yoga suits.

Richard: Mom, what are you wearing?

Sophia: My yoga suits. They're pretty, aren't they?

Richard: Ya, so you are practicing yoga?

Sophia: Yep. I joined the Women's Fitness Club and have been doing yoga for 2 weeks.

Richard: Good for you! How is it?

Sophia: I love it. Women's Fitness Club is the best fitness club for female in this city. All members, personal trainers and staff are woman. So there is no critical eye on you. I feel comfortable when I walk into the training room and meet women in different shapes.

Richard: Does the Club have various programs?

Sophia: Of course. There are different programs catering for different needs. For example, Body Balance is designed to tighten and strengthen the main muscle groups of your body. Yoga Class, which is the class I am in, is designed to alleviate stress, improve your energy level and achieve peaceful mind.

Richard: What makes you go to a yoga class?

Sophia: Well, it started about 3 weeks ago. I had very bad back pain. I took pain relief pills, but they didn't help much. One of my colleagues suggested that doing some yoga might help. So I tried several basic yoga poses. And they worked for me. That's why I joined the Yoga Class.

Richard: It sounds really good. So what do you do in the Yoga Class?

Sophia: We practice a set of poses and movements to re-establish mind-body connection through adjusting breath and stretching body. I show you one of the basic poses, "Mountain Position" which is designed to improve posture, balance and self-awareness. You can do this with me.

(Richard is following Sophia's instructions.)

Sophia: Stand with your feet together, hands at your sides, eyes looking forward. Raise your head up and lengthen the neck by lifting the base of your skull toward the ceiling. Balance your body. Breathe. Hold the posture, but try not to tense up. Now, inhale and slowly raise your arms over your head and hold for 5 to 10 seconds. Exhale and gently lower your arms to the original position. Hold for 5 to 10 seconds. Relax and repeat. Now, how do you feel?

Richard: I feel good. It's very refreshing.

Sophia: This is one of our warm-up exercises. It gives you a relaxed and energetic body for more complicated yoga movements. Are you interested in joining us?

Richard: Eh ... No thanks. It's too slow for me. I prefer strength training.

Dialogue D   Soccer Match

In the lift, Richard meets Mr. Mike Fang, a new employee working for the same company.

Mike: Morning, Richard, it seems you didn't have a good sleep last night.

Richard: Yea. I watched a soccer game on TV at midnight last night.

Mike: You mean the match of the FIFA World Cup?

Richard: Yes. It was a game not to be missed.

Mike: It was the final between Brazil and Italy, wasn't it?

Richard: Yes. It was the most exciting match I've ever seen. I wouldn't have missed it for anything! I thought both teams played superb with brilliant efforts from each side. Too bad one had to lose.

Mike: Who got the cup?

Richard: Brazil. They were evenly matched for almost the whole time. It could have gone either way!

Mike: What was the goal?

Richard: Four to three. The shot that decided everything in the last fifteen seconds was really something.

Mike: Which team is your favorite?

Richard: Brazil. They play as if they're dancing. They're the best players in the world, I believe. Say, Mike, what's your favorite sport?

Mike: Hmmm ... it's hard to say. I like golf a lot, but I guess I like tennis better.

Richard: Do you play much tennis?

Mike: Yes, quite a bit. How about a game sometime?

Richard: Sorry. I'm strictly a spectator ... soccer, baseball, basketball ... I watch them all.

Mike: Then maybe we can watch some soccer games together.

Richard: That would be awesome.

(A few weeks later. It's around half past three in the afternoon. Richard and his colleagues are having a coffee break. Mike comes into the open-plan office, holding high up some tickets in his right hand.)

Mike: Does anybody want to go to the soccer match this evening? I've got several spare tickets. They're good ones, too, for the grandstand.

David: Who're playing?

Mike: Shanghai Shenhua versus Manchester United.

David: Count me in. I'm a Manchester supporter! Are you coming, Richard?

Richard: I'm dying for a ticket.

David: How about you, Mary?

Mary: I'm not a big fan of soccer. But I can give you guys a lift to the stadium.

David: Great! What time shall we leave then? The kick-off is at 7.

Richard: There'll be a lot of traffic then. Let's say 6.

Mike: Perfect. We meet downstairs at 6.

(At the stadium.)

Richard: What a crowd! I didn't realize soccer was so popular in China.

David: It sure is. Manchester United is one of the top teams in Britain. So is Shanghai Shenhua in China. People would come from all over the country to watch a big match like this.

Mike: Come on guys. Follow me. We go in over there, Gate C. I hope we have a good view.

Richard: Who do you think would win this match, Mike?

Mike: Without David Beckham, Manchester United certainly has less power than before.

David: But I don't think Shenhua stands a chance against such a strong team, though.

Richard: It's too early to tell. We'll wait and see.

Notes

1.	varsity	大学
2.	alumni	(复)男毕业生;校友
3.	baseball	棒球
4.	softball	垒球
5.	rugby	橄榄球
6.	ice hockey	冰球
7.	cricket	板球
8.	rotund	圆肥的
9.	personal trainer	私人教练
10.	Roman Chair	罗马凳(锻炼背部肌肉的健身器材)
11.	back extension exercise	背部舒展运动
12.	erector spinae	竖脊肌
13.	gluteals	臀肌(可简称为 glutes)
14.	hamstrings	腿筋;大肌腱
15.	thigh	大腿
16.	hips are free to flex	髋关节可轻松弯曲
17.	spine	脊柱
18.	Back to business.	回到正题。
19.	use it or lose it	(身体)不用就会退步
20.	external obliques	外斜肌
21.	Breathe in on the descent.	在做向下动作时吸气
22.	You bet.	没错,当然;真的;的确(美国常用口语)
23.	treadmill	跑步机

24. But my abdomen feels sore.	不过，腹肌有点酸痛。
25. cool down	= warm down
26. 100 bpm	心率 100 次
27. prevent muscle cramps	防止肌肉痉挛
28. Yoga Class	瑜伽学习班
29. inhale	吸入
exhale	呼出
30. FIFA	国际足球联合会（简称来自法语：Federation Internationale de Football Association）
31. the final	决赛
32. I wouldn't have missed it for anything!	我错过什么也不会错过那场球赛。
33. Too bad one had to lose.	可惜总有一方得输。
34. they were evenly matched	双方势均力敌
35. It could have gone either way!	（双方）都有可能输或赢。
36. the shot that decided everything	那个决定胜负的一脚射门
37. How about a game sometime?	找时间赛一场如何？
38. I'm strictly a spectator.	我只当观众而已。
39. open-plan office	敞开式办公室
40. spare tickets	余票
41. grandstand	正面看台
42. versus	对抗
43. The kick-off is at 7.	开赛时间是 7 点。
44. stand a chance against	击败……的机会

Functional Expressions

Expressing Curiosity

1. Can someone tell me about the results of the tennis semifinal?
2. Do you happen to know when the next race begins?
3. Does anyone know what's going on in that country?
4. I don't suppose you know who won the game?
5. I hope you don't mind me asking, but are they from Argentina?
6. I wish I knew more about the marathon.
7. I wish someone would tell me about his mysterious disappearance.
8. I wonder if you could tell me the reason he didn't show up in cycling.
9. I wouldn't mind knowing who won the men's 100 m run.

10. I'd give a lot to know about the winning team in women's soccer.

11. I'd like to know how they managed to win the World Cup.

12. If only I knew about that!

13. The store's still open，I suppose?

14. What I'd really like to find out is the result of that competition.

15. What's in your mind?

Stating You Are Pleased

1. Fantastic!

2. Great!

3. How wonderful!

4. I'm very pleased.

5. Oh，that's marvelous.

6. Smashing!

7. Super!

8. Terrific!

9. That's good news.

10. That's the best news I've heard for a long time.

11. That's the best thing I've heard in years.

Reproaching Somebody

1. Are you mad，Tom?

2. Are you nuts?

3. Aren't you ashamed of your selfish behavior?

4. Can't you be serious for once?

5. For shame!

6. How could you be so rude?

7. Now look what you've done!

8. Shame on you!

9. What do you think you are doing?

Telling Somebody to Hurry

1. Get a move on!

2. Hurry!

3. I think you'd better get going.

4. Let's get going.

5. Make haste!

6. Quick!

7. Speed up!

8. Step on it!

9. We'd better hurry.

 Communicative Task

Beijing 2008 Olympics

Types of Task: group, class.

Functions Practiced: exchanging information, expressing curiosity, describing events, stating you are pleased or disappointed, making comments.

Pre-task

1. Select one in your pair to read the following message to the other.

Every two years the Olympics (Summer Games and Winter Games) capture our attention like no other sporting event. The Games, especially the Summer Games, make front-page news, magazine covers, and prime-time television. During the Games, there are more 300 channels broadcasting the Olympic Games to 220 countries and territories, with 35,000 hours of dedicated coverage (2,000 per day). An estimated 3.6 billion people (unduplicated) accessed the images of the Sydney 2000 Games; 3.9 billion people watched the Athens 2004 Games and 4.8 billion people viewed Beijing 2008 Olympics on television worldwide.

2. If you are the one to read the message, now ask your pair two questions about the Olympics.

3. Now work on your own to recall some KEY FACTS about Beijing 2008 Olympics and fill out the blanks below.

Opening date: _____

Closing date: _____

Country of the host city: _____

Candidate cities: _____ , _____ , _____ and _____

4. Some events are listed below, in case that you might not be familiar with the terms in English.

10 km walk	4×400 meter relay	discus	equestrian
archery	hammer throw	javelin	fencing
badminton	synchronized swimming	softball	kayaking
boxing	field hockey	rowing	water polo
canoeing	long jump	judo	weightlifting
cycling	shot putting	hurdles	pentathlon
decathlon	heptathlon	diving	yachting

5. Beijing 2008 Olympics created 35 sport pictograms that represent the 28 Olympic sports and certain disciplines. They were the essential visual reference for any information related to the competition schedule and the venues. Each of them was a separate image showing the sports and disciplines' special features and enabling the viewer to recognize them immediately. Can you recognize the following pictograms and the related sports?

6. Recall all the sporting events you watched on television and the relevant information about the Games，and fill out the following grid.

The Olympic Games I Know

Beijing 2008 Olympics

The _____ Summer Olympic Games

Attendance：_____ nations

Males：_____ Females：_____ （Number of Athletes）

Most-medaled Team：_____

China's Rank：_____

Events I watched	Medalists	Events I watched	Medalists

Task Procedure

1. Compare your filled-out grid and other information with your classmates in your group and discuss them if some of your answers are not identical.

2. Now take the grid with you and find your fellow students who watched same events on television in your class, noticing how to start and close a conversation, and how to take up a point.

3. Ask your fellow students who have watched same sporting events to sit around a desk to recall the most spectacular scenes when sports history has been made.

4. Recall and discuss the moments you felt most excited, worried or disappointed for our national team's performance in the Beijing 2008 Olympic Games.

5. Exchange your comments with your fellow students on both Chinese and foreign athletes you both like most or dislike somewhat.

6. In your group select one Chinese athlete as the most valuable player favored by all your group members.

7. Report your unanimous decision to your class, providing reasons to support your decision if necessary.

Extra Information:

Official Website: http://en. beijing2008. cn/

Events Held at Beijing 2008 Olympics

Swimming	Diving	Synchronized Swimming	Water Polo
Archery	Athletics	Badminton	Baseball
Basketball	Boxing	Wrestling	Canoe/Kayak Slalom
Cycling	Equestrian	Fencing	Football
Artistic Gymnastics	Rhythmic Gymnastics	Trampoline	Handball
Hockey	Judo	Modern Pentathlon	Rowing
Sailing	Shooting	Softball	Table Tennis
Taekwondo	Tennis	Triathlon	Volleyball
Beach Volleyball	Weightlifting		

Unit Fifteen

Entertainment

 **Warm Up**

1. Say out Loud and Fast

1) About 80% of all American TV entertainment comes from Hollywood.

2) I love the rides and the food at amusement parks.

3) If you don't shake a leg, we're going to be late for the movie.

4) He is determined to get a ticket for the ballet even if it means standing all night.

5) While Mike was an only child, he would amuse himself with his toys.

6) Monkey is a general mascot and a target of amusement.

7) Businessmen often entertain their guests in the restaurant.

8) Tom Cruise's entertainment career has spanned nearly 25 years.

9) Cycling is also a form of entertainment and recreation.

10) The child was entertaining himself with his building blocks.

2. Culture Tip

In the United States there is no national television as there is in China and the United Kingdom. All the stations are run commercially. Companies sponsor shows and pay for advertising and thus have a lot of influence over what is being shown on TV. If the show they are sponsoring is unpopular or the channel they are paying for advertising is not up to the scratch then they will withdraw their support. Advertising is so prevalent that pictures of America's new president taking the solemn oath of office may share the same air time as an advert for an electric can opener.

In many areas of the US, television is broadcast 24 hours a day on 50 channels or more. ABC, CBS, NBC, CNN and the sports channel, SPCN are the more famous nationwide channels. But in the UK, there are just five channels — BBC1, BBC2, ITV (Independent Television), Channel 4 and Channel 5 — on terrestrial television. The BBC is paid by a TV license system where each television set owner has to pay £80 a year. Though the BBC is responsible to the British government it tends to have a maverick, independent attitude. Quality is emphasized in the UK and schedules are set for the public's convenience and are easy to remember.

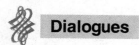 **Dialogues**

Dialogue A   Digital TV

Richard is in Melbourne, Australia on a business trip now. He runs into an old friend of his, John Miller.

John: Hi, Richard. I haven't seen you for ages. How have you been?

Richard: How nice to see you again, buddy. I've been up north on a business trip for a couple of weeks. How are you going?

John: Not too bad, but ...

Richard: What's the matter?

John: Look, my dad called me a few weeks ago. He is living in a small town in Tasmania. The local government decides to switch from analog TV to digital TV.

Richard: Well. That's great. Your father can enjoy the benefits of new technology and better quality pictures and sound.

John: Richard, I know that. What makes me a bit uneasy is I may have to take a few days off and go down there to help him with the switchover, because they are aged and may get something wrong.

Richard: I guess you have to. I know you are busy with your term paper. And I also know what keeps you down. TV programs, whether talk shows, dramas, or sitcoms, are awfully boring, except the sports channels on live. Even the documentaries on ABC, CBS, NBC, CNN and BBC are boring, too. Once you watch one, you will find it on the other channels again the next day, next month and next year.

John: You really know me a lot. But my parents love soap operas. They would watch anything played on telly.

Richard: They are retired, and have not much to do. I guess TV becomes a part of their daily lives, like many aged ones.

John:	Guess what else makes me not enthusiastic about the switchover?
Richard:	Well, it must be the cost, I suppose.
John:	Right! Look, this is the brochure from the local Digital Switchover Taskforce.
Richard:	The brochure looks nice.
John:	Yes, it does. But after you read the contents inside, you might change your mind. It will cost you at least 35 dollars more every month, if you decide to go digital.
Richard:	That much?
John:	It lists the fees in the brochure. Read page 4, please. Yes, right here. Under "Your Choice".
Richard:	(*Reading the brochure.*) ... assist you in making ... the most informed, cost-friendly and appropriate decision ... when switching to digital TV.
John:	Look at the cheapest charge for digital channel at the bottom line. It will cost me 35 dollars more every month, if my parents decide to switch. This is way too much.
Richard:	It is. I am afraid that is why most people won't like being forced to upgrade. But I guess you have no choice. It says, in six months, the whole areas of this country will switch from analog TV to Digital TV.
John:	Yes. That's something for sure, unless my parents cut off their addiction to TV and find new ways of entertainment.
Richard:	That's impossible, I am afraid.
John:	You are right and I do not intend to do that. After all digital is digital, much better than analog. I just hate the phrase they use.
Richard:	What is it?
John:	Look here, "Cost-friendly". Is it a friendly cost? I'm fed up with all this nonsense.
Richard:	Well, this is business. They have to use some nice words to comfort the customers and soothe their upset emotions.

Dialogue B   A Deal

After two weeks hard working for the exams, Isabel and Tina, Isabel's best friend and roommate, decide that they deserve a night out in town.

Isabel:	Tina, we've been hard at exams for two weeks. So why don't we take it easy this evening?
Tina:	Great! What do you suggest?

Isabel:	How about seeing a play? I know *Hamlet* is on at the Grand Hall.
Tina:	I'll go along with that. Who's playing Hamlet?
Isabel:	Mike Paul. Have you heard of him?
Tina:	Yes, he's one of Britain's best Shakespearean actors.
Isabel:	There are two performances every day. Does 7 o'clock suit you?
Tina:	Sure thing.
Isabel:	Would you like seats in the stalls or in the dress circle?
Tina:	I prefer the stalls. As near to the stage as possible. Say, the fourth or fifth row.
Isabel:	(*Looking in the newspaper.*) Dear me! I got the wrong date. There's no performance at the Grand Hall tonight. But we could go to the cinema instead.
Tina:	What's on?
Isabel:	Let me see ... um, *Just for Fun* ... that sounds interesting. There are several screenings this evening. Do you want to go to the late show or the earlier one?
Tina:	I fancy going to the late show at 11.
Isabel:	You must be joking. Then we'll be back after midnight!
Tina:	Why not? The exams are all over. Just relax and enjoy!
Isabel:	OK, anything you say and you win. But the tickets are on you.
Tina:	It's a deal!
Isabel:	And a nice restaurant before the show, too.
Tina:	Oh, come on. Isabel, I'll go bankrupt overnight.
Isabel:	Don't worry. Tomorrow's breakfast is on me.

Dialogue C   3D TV

Mr. White is renovating their home and thinking about creating a home entertainment center with a new TV. Mrs. White plans to buy a 52 inch HD TV. However, after Mr. White tells her that 3D TV is available now, she decides to go to GOME to check it out. Terry, the shop assistant, is with her.

Terry:	Good afternoon, can I help you with anything?
Mrs. White:	Yes. I want to know more about 3D TV. Do you have any information booklet I can read?
Terry:	I am really sorry that I don't have printouts to give you. We used to have a booklet for each 3D TV. But I am more than happy to answer any question you have.

Mrs. White: Oh, OK. How come a flat screen TV can show 3D pictures?

Terry: Well, all 3D TV works on the same principle which mimics how human eyes create three dimensional images. Pictures are taken from two cameras: one from your left eye angle and another from your right eye angle. When the TV combines the images, just like what your brain does, it will appear three dimensional.

Mrs. White: Oh, I see. Why we need to wear 3D glasses?

Terry: This is the tricky part. If you can come with me, I will show you a 3D TV. I can explain this better.

(Mrs. White and Terry are standing in front of a 3D TV showing a 3D program.)

Terry: You probably have noticed that the 3D program is not as clear as 2D TV program. But if you can put on this pair of glasses, you can see the difference.

(Mrs. White puts the glasses on.)

Mrs. White: Yes, it's 3D! It's amazing!

Terry: Remember I said earlier that two images are taken from different angles. What TV does is to combine the two images into one and display it on a 2D TV screen. What the 3D glasses do is to block out one of the two combined images; so each eye only sees one angle of the same image at a time. Because the refresh rate is so high that your brain treats the flicking images as continuous pictures flow.

Mrs. White: I reckon the higher the refresh rate, the smoother the image.

Terry: That's right!

Mrs. White: I am thinking about creating an entertainment center at home. How big do you think a TV should be for the best viewing experience?

Terry: Well, it's up to you. It depends on how big the room is and how much you want to spend. The smallest 3D TV we have is 46″. We also have 50″, 54″, 58″, 63″ and 65″.

Mrs. White: Is there any particular brand you would suggest?

Terry: For 3D TV, we have Panasonic, Sony, LG and Samsung available in store now. For the best 3D effects, Panasonic is the one I recommend. However, there is only one problem with this TV. It only displays 3D effects on Blu-ray 3D program. In other words, if the program is not 3D, it won't show 3D.

Mrs. White: Are there a lot of 3D programs available now?

Terry: I afraid not a lot of them. This is one of the problems when we promote 3D TV. However, the good news is that TVs from the other three brands have the capability to convert normal 2D programs to 3D. They have what's called built-in "conversion engine" which can create 3D effects from 2D images.

Mrs. White: Sounds interesting ... but I have to wear the glasses, right?

Terry: Yes, you do. Normally we sell glasses separately. This week, all LG TVs are on sale with 15% discount and you can get 2 pairs of 3D glasses for free when you buy any LG 3D TV.

Mrs. White: Do the glasses use battery?

Terry: The free ones use battery. Each battery has up to 60 hours of viewing time and costs about 25 *yuan* each. We have rechargeable glasses as well. But they are for sale separately and more expensive.

Mrs. White: Thank you very much for your help. I will talk to my husband tonight and then decide what to buy.

Terry: My pleasure. This is my business card. If you have any question, just give me a call.

Dialogue D   Go Balling

On the campus Tina is trying to persuade Isabel to go dancing with her.

Tina: Isabel, I've got good news for you.

Isabel: What is it?

Tina: There's a ball this evening.

Isabel: Who cares?

Tina: What's wrong with you? We haven't gone dancing for a long time.

Isabel: So what?

Tina: We must go to a dance tonight, or we'll forget how to dance.

Isabel: Yes. But what do you expect me to wear?

Tina: I see. Your blue dress is quite nice.

Isabel: Oh, just forget about it. I wore it at your birthday party last month. And I've got no jewel to match.

Tina: Come on. Don't be a stick-in-the-mud. Why don't you wear a red rose? It would go with the blue dress perfectly.

Isabel: Maybe you're right. I hope a red rose would make me feel better.

Tina: Oh, I almost forget. Could you lend me your white shoes? Mine need repairing.

Isabel: No problem.

Tina: Are you going to put some makeup on?

Isabel:	Don't ask me! I can't afford those expensive cosmetics.
Tina:	Neither can I. What if no boys come to invite us?
Isabel:	Then we'll have to be a couple of wallflowers!
Tina:	You'll have to kill me first!
Isabel:	Why don't we ask some boys to go with us?
Tina:	But the boys I know are not good dancers. They'll spoil your shoes. It's worse than being wallflowers!
Isabel:	You're right.
Tina:	I remember a couple of boys in the Rural Economics Department dance quite well and one of them actually called you before we had exams. Why don't you give him a call?
Isabel:	OK. I'll give a try. Pass me the phone and the address book under it, please.

Notes

1. not up to the scratch	没有达到规定的要求
2. so prevalent	无处不在
3. taking the solemn oath of office	庄严宣誓就职
4. same air time	同一播出时间
5. an electric can opener	电动开罐器
6. ABC(American Broadcasting Company)	美国广播公司
7. CBS(Columbia Broadcasting Company)	(美国)哥伦比亚广播公司
8. NBC(National Broadcasting Company)	(美国)国家广播公司
9. CNN(Cable News Network)	(美国)有线新闻网
10. BBC(British Broadcasting Corporation)	英国广播公司
11. SPCN(Sports Pro Community Network)	(美国)体育电视台
12. terrestrial television	地面电视(不用卫星传送讯号)
13. maverick，independent attitude	特立独行的态度
14. I haven't seen you for ages.	好久不见。
15. buddy	(口语)哥们儿,同伴,搭档,朋友
16. analog TV	模拟电视
17. digital TV	数字电视
18. switchover	转换,切换(如顺序、方向、流向等)
19. talk show	谈话节目,脱口秀
20. sitcom	室内情景连续剧
21. on live	电视直播

22. documentary	纪录片
23. soap operas	肥皂剧
24. telly(television)	电视
25. brochure	小册子
26. taskforce	(为完成某项任务成立的)机构/工作组
27. I'm fed up with all this nonsense.	我受够了(烦死了)这些废话。
28. soothe	缓和
29. stalls	剧院正厅前座
30. dress circle	剧院二楼前座
31. several screenings this evening	今晚有好几场
32. But the tickets are on you.	那么你买票。
33. It's a deal!	就这么定了。
34. bankrupt	破产
35. GOME	国美电器
36. mimic	仿效,模仿
37. three dimensional image	三维图像
38. tricky part	奥妙之处
39. block out	遮挡住了
40. refresh rate	刷新频率
41. conversion engine	(图像)转换引擎
42. So what?	那又怎么样?
43. stick-in-the-mud	挑剔;易挑剔的人
44. It would go with the blue dress perfectly.	它很配那条蓝裙子。
45. a couple of wallflowers	一对局外人
46. You'll have to kill me first!	你还不如先杀了我吧!

 Functional Expressions

Feeling Bored

1. Bother it!
2. Can't work up much enthusiasm for anything today.
3. How boring!
4. I don't find the sports channel very exciting.
5. I don't think the comedy show is very interesting, actually.
6. I'm afraid I find it difficult to be enthusiastic about this video game.
7. I'm cheesed off with his jokes.

8. I'm fed up with all this nonsense.

9. I'm not at all keen on that sort of entertainment.

10. I'm rather bored by that rumor about the actress.

11. I'm sorry, but the waltz rather bores me.

12. I'm tired of it, the same old story over and over again.

13. Isn't it a bother?

14. It was a bit of a bore, wasn't it?

15. It was awfully boring.

16. That fellow's manner really turns me off.

17. To be quite frank, I find this local opera rather tedious.

18. Traveling during rush hour can be a bit of a bind.

19. What a bother having to climb stairs home.

Believing

1. I believe that man.

2. I believe what you said.

3. I can trust his account of what happened.

4. I can well believe that.

5. I feel confident of his ability to perform in this concert.

6. I have perfect trust in my friend John.

7. I'll take your word for it.

8. It seems credible.

9. Seems believable.

Disbelieving

1. Are you kidding me?

2. Did you really?

3. Do you think I'd believe a story like that?

4. Don't expect me to believe you.

5. Don't pull my leg.

6. How is that possible?

7. I don't believe a word of it.

8. I don't buy your story.

9. I find that hard to believe.

10. I know better than that!

11. Is that so?

12. It can't be true.

13. It's too good to be true.

14. Oh, yeah?

15. That story isn't good enough for me.

16. That's a good one. (Sarcasm)

17. You can't be serious.

18. You can't expect me to believe that.

19. You don't mean that, surely.

20. You must be joking.

21. You're joking.

22. You're not serious, are you?

 Communicative Task

My Favorite Director

Types of Task: pair, group, class.

Functions Practiced: telling others your habits, expressing you feeling bored, retelling a movie story, expressing other's favorites.

Pre-task

1. We all know that there are moments during the day when we have nothing to do, and no plans, for example, when you are waiting for a teacher, a friend, and so on. How do you occupy these periods of time, either mentally or physically? For example, here is a list of what most people do during the TV commercials.

During TV commercials most people are ...

Talking to others	Rushing to do the washing-up
Reading something or anything	Getting up and do something else
Going to the bathroom	Changing channels
Looking for something to eat or read	Calling a friend
Watering the plants	Brushing their teeth

2. Recall what you and your family members usually do during the TV commercials and write down your recalling below.

1) _____

_____

2) _____

_____

3) _____

_____

3. Tell your pair how you kill time during the TV advertisements.

4. Exchange ideas with your pair on habitual ways of killing time when you feel bored.

5. Tell your pair what you usually do during school breaks in summer and winter. Ask your pair for the alternatives to spend long holiday.

6. Fetch for extra ideas from your pair about what she/he regularly does to kill the time when she/he is：

1) on a bus

2) in a lift/elevator

3) in a doctor's waiting-room

4) in an airport/train station/bus stop

5) at a supermarket check-out

6) getting your hair done/cut

7) waiting for the film/play to begin in a cinema/theatre

8) during the class breaks

Task Procedure

1. Ask your pair if she/he is a regular moviegoer? Ask your pair who is her/his favorite movie director?

2. Follow the examples provided in the table **Samples of My Favorite Directors and Movies**, and fill out the movies your pair recalls in the table **My Pair's Favorite Directors and Movies**.

Samples of My Favorite Directors and Movies

Directors	Movies
Feng Xiaogang	*The Banquet*（2006） *The Assembly*（2007） *If You Are The One*（2008） *Aftershock*（2010） *If You Are The One II*（2010）
Zhang Yimou	*Hero*（2002） *House of Flying Daggers*（2004） *Riding Alone for Thousands of Miles*（2005） *Curse of the Golden Flower*（2006） *A Simple Noodle Story*（2009）

My Pair's Favorite Directors and Movies

Director	Movies

3. Ask your pair to select one of her/his favorite movies and tell you the synopsis of the movie. A format of movie synopsis is provided below for your reference.

Dreams Come True

This movie is the first Happy-New-Year production ever made in the Chinese mainland and features seven "daydreams" created by four youths Yao Yuan, Zhou Beiyan, Qian Kang and Liang Zi. They offer customers a special service, which is called *Dreams Come True for One Day*.

Their service wins public favor after many twists and turns. However, the four young staff members find they have not made much money, as they often help others realize their dreams without asking for payment.

At last, the four youths decide to turn the service into a charitable one, not a profit-making business. The film ends with the cheerful wedding ceremony of Yao and Zhou.

4. Now listen carefully to your pair's version of this movie synopsis. Make notes, if necessary.

5. Reverse your roles from step 3.

6. After both of you finish the movie synopsis, go to your group and retell the group members your synopsis of the movies.

7. In your group, after the retelling activity, make comments on the popular movies in the past twelve months and vote to decide who in China should be nominated for the worst actor and actress of the year.

8. Report to your class your group's decision and reasons.

Unit Sixteen

Birthday and Holiday

 Warm Up

1. Say out Loud and Fast

1) Some people consider a nice vacation to be staying near a pleasant beach or in a secluded cabin.

2) Do you love the thought of being able to explore the places you've only read about in books?

3) Why not experience sightseeing adventure travel at a destination you have always dreamed of going to?

4) Seasickness can take the fun out of the best cruises and whale watching tours, preventing you from enjoying your holiday.

5) I write love letters to all those I feel close to — and maybe some I'd like to feel closer to.

6) Birthdays are to celebrate another year on the planet and a great excuse to spoil someone you love, or splurge on yourself!

7) A long weekend at a lake resort, a one night stay at a theme park, and a spa weekend are all popular birthday ideas.

8) Many twenty-first birthday party ideas are filled with ways to celebrate adulthood in America.

9) If there is one holiday that every person in the world shares, no matter their religious backgrounds or beliefs, it is the birthday.

10) The birthday cake is the apex of the party and the decorations are almost as important as the theme of the party itself.

2. Culture Tip

Christmas and New Year are the most well-known Western holidays and are generally celebrated throughout the world. Christmas is a time for big dinners and gift exchanging; New Year is just a big party and no gifts are needed. But there are a lot more holidays.

In the United States, Independence Day, Thanksgiving Day and Labor Day are three major holidays. Parades and big firework display characterize the Independence Day while you may see parades only on Labor Day. In a sense, Thanksgiving Day is more or less the same as the traditional Chinese Spring Festival on which families get together and a large meal is served to mark the end of the farming season or the beginning of the new farming season ahead.

In the United Kingdom and Australia, holidays are more religiously based. Therefore, Easter is an occasion for people to swap chocolate or painted hard boiled eggs to remember Jesus Christ's Crucifixion and Resurrection.

One more occasion on which people give presents is for the birth of a baby when the parents come home with their newly born child. Presents are usually baby clothes and toys, and the usual thing to do is to say how cute the baby is and ponder over to which of the relations the child looks most similar.

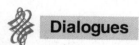

Dialogues

Dialogue A   Isabel's Birthday Party

Today is Isabel's birthday. She holds a birthday party in her dorm. Andrew, one of Isabel's friends, comes to the party.

Andrew:	Happy birthday, Isabel! You look great today!
Isabel:	Thank you. I'm glad you managed to come.
Andrew:	Here is my present for you.
Isabel:	Thank you. It looks great. What's in it?
Andrew:	Open it.
Isabel:	A musical box! It's my favorite song! How nice of you, Andrew!
Andrew:	Glad you like it. Oh, there is a band in the room. How nice! What an exciting party! I like it.
Isabel:	Thank you! My parents invited them for me. That's their present.
Andrew:	How great! Look at that drummer. How smart he plays! I can't help dancing to the music.
Isabel:	It seems you're crazy about drumming. You want to be a drummer, don't you?
Andrew:	Yes, that's my dream. I'm dying for a set of drums. What about you?

Isabel: Me? Well, I want to be an overseas correspondent, so I can travel around the world for free.

Andrew: But that's dangerous. Working is different from traveling, especially for a correspondent. You have to face the hunger, drought, floods, and even wars.

Isabel: I know. That's exactly what attracts me. I want to experience all that exists in the world. People don't live only to enjoy life.

Andrew: It sounds you've grown into woman overnight. OK. Make a wish before you blow the candles out. It'll come true.

Isabel: An old story.

Andrew: But it does work!

Isabel: Does it? Oh, forget about it. Help yourself to some drinks.

Andrew: Isabel? I ... I wonder if you could leave the first dance for me.

Isabel: Sorry. I've already promised John the first two.

Andrew: I knew I should have asked earlier.

Isabel: Go and ask Tina. She isn't engaged yet.

Dialogue B   Chinese Traditional Festivals

Mrs. White chats with her Chinese friend, Mrs. Yulan Wang, with an intention to know more about Chinese culture.

Yulan: Mrs. White, tomorrow is the first of October, our National Day.

Sophia: My sincere congratulations on your National Day. By the way, how many days do you celebrate for this public holiday?

Yulan: Three days, statutory and plus four weekends. Seven days altogether. From the 1st to the 7th. And we call it Golden Week.

Sophia: How do you celebrate this holiday?

Yulan: In past times, the central government will hold military parades, political gatherings and speeches in Tian'anmen Square. Since 2000, with the strong economy growth, the National Day is celebrated with a variety of government-organized festivities, including fireworks and concerts throughout the whole country. Public places, such as People's Square in Shanghai, are decorated in a festive theme.

Sophia: Then what do you usually do during this holiday?

Yulan: Visit relatives or take time for traveling. But this year, I decided to do something different. I'll perform at the Peoples' Square with my friends and be part of the celebration.

Sophia: That's wonderful! What other holidays do you have in fall?

Yulan: We have the Moon Festival or Mid-autumn Day on the 15th of the eighth month in the Chinese lunar calendar. The moon is believed to be at its brightest that night.

Sophia: It sounds very poetic. Do you have any traditional food for that day?

Yulan: It's a tradition for Chinese people to eat moon cakes during this festival.

Sophia: What are moon cakes?

Yulan: They're little round cakes shaped liked a full moon.

Sophia: What're they made of?

Yulan: They're made of flour, sugar, oil, eggs, and so on.

Sophia: What's in it?

Yulan: Oh, various stuffings. There're dried and preserved fruits, walnuts, sweetmeat, salted eggs, and so on. But nowadays, some young people don't like moon cakes any longer, as they're too sweet and oily.

Sophia: That's true. People prefer lightly flavored food nowadays. It's good for health. I saw a special Chinese food of that kind yesterday.

Yulan: What's it like?

Sophia: It is sticky rice wrapped up in reed leaves in the shape of a triangle, with sugar, meat or dates inside.

Yulan: I see. That's Zongzi. There are many different kinds of Zongzi, each with a particular flavor. We mainly eat them on the fifth day of the fifth month of the Chinese lunar calendar.

Sophia: Is it a festival?

Yulan: Yes. It's the Dragon Boat Festival and now it's one of the statutory holidays. Originally, it is to commemorate Qu Yuan, a famous Chinese poet from the kingdom of Chu, who died for his country. It's also a custom to row dragon boats and eat Zongzi on that day.

Sophia: Dragon boats? I watched dragon boats race in Guangdong last year. It was fabulous. Any other public holidays?

Yulan: Yes, we have several other official public holidays, for instance, New Year's Day, Spring Festival, International Labor Day, and Qingming Festival on April 4th or 5th.

Sophia: Thank you for your information, May I invite you to deliver a presentation on Chinese holidays at our monthly seminar in our agency? You know, most of our staff just came from the States. They need know more about China.

Yulan: That'll be my honor. Give me a call one week ahead of your seminar. I must get myself well prepared.

Sophia: OK. My secretary will call you a week before our seminar.

Dialogue C   Spring Festival and Christmas

Sophia comes across Mrs. Lirong Liu on her way home.

Sophia: Mrs. Liu, how are you doing?

Lirong: I'm quite busy. You know, the Spring Festival is drawing near.

Sophia: The Spring Festival? That's the Chinese Lunar New Year, isn't it?

Lirong: Yes. It's always one month or so later than the New Year's Day.

Sophia: How do Chinese people celebrate it?

Lirong: Usually, the whole family gets together and has a big feast on the Eve of the Lunar New Year. During the following days, people pay visits to their relatives and friends. Nowadays, more and more people like to go traveling with the family during the Spring Festival, which officially lasts 7 days, while some would rather stay at home, watching TV or visiting friends living in the same city.

Sophia: Are there any special traditional customs?

Lirong: Yes. Among the other dishes, a whole fish must be served for the dinner on the Eve of the Lunar New Year, and the family members can eat up all the dishes except for the fish.

Sophia: Why?

Lirong: Chinese people always love a pun with their language because there are so many homonyms in the Chinese language. The pronunciation of fish in Chinese applies to another Chinese character, which means abundance. So when serving a whole fish, the host means to wish the recipients year after year of abundance.

Sophia: It sounds interesting! Do you exchange gifts?

Lirong: No. Instead, the elders give the children each a red packet filled with new bank notes.

Sophia: Can children use the money as they like?

Lirong: Of course. That's why they are always longing for the Spring Festival.

Sophia: The same with Americans. Before Christmas, the department stores are crowded with those who rack their brains to buy suitable gifts for families. Some complain that they are using the money that belongs to the future to buy gifts to those who don't need them at all!

Lirong: That's true everywhere in the world. Holidays are the time to spend money. On the other hand, it seems modern people can't live without holidays.

Sophia: I couldn't agree more with your incisive comment on holidays. Your observation is penetrating and brilliant.

Lirong: Thank you. I think the essence of the Spring Festival is for the whole family to get together and have fun. In China, no matter how far away from home, the family members are bound to come back before the dinner at the eve of the New Year, just as the old saying goes, "East or west, home is best."

Sophia: Yes, I learned it is very difficult to get a train ticket during the Spring Festival for those migrant workers. Well, I enjoyed very much talking to you.

Lirong: Me, too. See you.

Sophia: Bye now.

Dialogue D   Christmas Dinner

The Whites have invited Mr. Guangtian Wang and Mrs. Yulan Wang to come over to celebrate Christmas with them.

Henry: Have some more turkey please, Mr. Wang.

Guangtian: No, thanks. I am really full. It's delicious, but I've eaten too much already.

Henry: How about you, Mrs. Wang?

Yulan: No, thank you. I know there's Christmas pudding next.

Sophia: Right. Pudding will be ready in a few more minutes.

Guangtian: Americans also have turkey on Thanksgiving, don't they?

Sophia: Yes. The table is heaped with roast stuffed turkey, baked sweet potatoes, corn, pumpkin pie, and plum pudding.

Yulan: What's Thanksgiving for?

Sophia: It was the day on which the Pilgrims had a celebration to give thanks for a good harvest in North America many years ago.

Henry: That's why it is celebrated primarily in the United States and Canada. While there was an underlying religious element in the original celebration, Thanksgiving today is primarily identified as a secular holiday.

Sophia: In Canada, Thanksgiving is celebrated on the second Monday of October and we, in the United States, celebrate it on the fourth Thursday of November.

Yulan: That'll be a bit difficult for me to memorize the dates.

Guangtian: I wonder if it is the cold weather in Canada that made them to celebrate it almost 6 weeks earlier.

Henry: Could be. I never tried to find the cause, though. What I do know is Thanksgiving in Canada falls on the same day as Columbus Day in the United States.

Yulan： How do you celebrate it?

Henry： It was and still is an indigenous holiday. Thanksgiving is a day when the American family renews its gratitude for freedom to live. It's a family-type affair. Everyone stuffs himself with food.

Yulan： You can also find scarecrows and black cats at a Thanksgiving Party, can't you?

Henry： No，you're mixed up with Halloween.

Guangtian： What's that?

Sophia： It's mostly for kids. They dress up in ghost costumes and knock at neighborhood doors and shout "Trick or Treat!"

Yulan： What does it mean?

Sophia： That means "You must treat us with candies，or we'll play tricks on you." Such as，breaking the windows，but that never really happens，since it would be against the law.

Yulan： That's interesting. What day is it?

Sophia： The last day of October. Halloween is an annual holiday observed on October 31，but not a public holiday. Excuse me，I go and check the pudding. It should be ready.

Henry： I still remember the activities I enjoyed in my childhood，such as trick-or-treat，costume parties，visiting haunted attractions，telling scary stories，and watching horror movies.

Sophia： (*Back from kitchen with pudding*.) I also enjoyed carving jack-o'-lanterns, bonfires, apple bobbing, and playing pranks. Now try this Christmas pudding.

Yulan： Mmmmm，it's great. I like the flavors of cinnamon and nutmeg. You must give me the recipe.

Sophia： No problem. But I'm not sure if all the ingredients are available in Shanghai.

Yulan： No worry, I can use substitutes.

Sophia： OK. But I don't guarantee the right flavor if you use substitutes.

Yulan： As long as my daughter don't mind.

Sophia： I know. She is crazy for anything sweet.

Notes

1. swap chocolate	互赠巧克力
2. hard boiled eggs	煮熟透了的鸡蛋
3. Jesus Christ's Crucifixion and Resurrection	耶稣基督的受难和复活

4. How smart he plays!	他演奏得多么潇洒!
5. I'm dying for a set of drums.	我非常想得到一套鼓。
6. an overseas correspondent	驻外记者
7. People don't live only to enjoy life.	人活着并不仅仅为了享受生活。
8. It sounds you've grown into woman overnight.	这话听起来就像你一夜之间就长大成人了。
9. an old story	老生常谈
10. I've promised John the first two.	我已经答应与约翰跳头两场舞。
11. She isn't engaged yet.	她还没答应和谁跳呢。
12. It sounds very poetic.	听上去很有诗意。
13. various stuffings	各种馅料
14. sweetmeat	蜜饯
15. lightly flavored	口味清淡
16. sticky rice	糯米
17. reed leave	芦苇叶
18. dates	大枣
19. the Dragon Boat Festival	端午节
20. statutory holiday	法定假日
21. to commemorate Qu Yuan	纪念屈原
22. deliver a presentation	作报告
23. the States(the United States)	美国
24. feast	盛宴
25. pun	双关语
26. recipient	(本文中)被请的人;受者(体)
27. abundance	丰裕
28. red packet	红包
29. rack their brains	绞尽脑汁,挖空心思
30. can't live without holidays	生活中离不开假日
31. incisive comment	凌厉的评论
32. Your observation is penetrating and brilliant.	你的洞察力深刻又敏锐。
33. East or west, home is best.	金窝银窝,不如自己的草窝。
34. Pilgrims	朝圣者(最初去美洲的移民)
35. an underlying religious element	一个隐含的宗教元素
36. a secular holiday	一个世俗的节日
37. an indigenous holiday	一个当地人的节日
38. Halloween	万圣节前夕
39. It's mostly for kids.	主要是孩子们的节日。

40.	against the law	触犯法律
41.	carving jack-o'-lanterns	雕刻南瓜灯笼
42.	bonfires, apple bobbing, and playing pranks	点篝火、用嘴叼苹果和搞恶作剧
43.	cinnamon and nutmeg	桂皮与肉豆蔻
44.	substitute	替代品

 Functional Expressions

Giving General Good Wishes

1. All the best in your new job.
2. All the very best with your family.
3. Enjoy yourself!
4. Every success in your business.
5. Good luck in the exam.
6. Good luck to you!
7. Have a good time.
8. Have fun.
9. Hope things go all right with you.
10. I hope everything goes well.
11. I hope you have a good time.
12. I hope you'll get over it soon.
13. I hope you'll get well tomorrow.
14. I wish Mr. Mayor and all our friends a good health!
15. I wish this conference a complete success!
16. I wish you success.
17. May you succeed.
18. Please give my best wishes to your parents.
19. The best of luck.
20. The very best of luck with you.

Responding to General Good Wishes

1. Many thanks.
2. Thank you very much.
3. Thank you.
4. Thanks, Jane.

Giving Good Wishes on a Special Occasion
1. A happy New Year.
2. A merry Christmas.
3. Happy anniversary!
4. Happy birthday!
5. Happy Easter!
6. Happy Valentine!
7. Have a good Christmas!
8. Many happy returns.

Responding to Good Wishes on a Special Occasion
1. Thank you very much. Same to you!
2. Thank you. And the same to you!
3. Thanks. And you too!
4. Thanks. The same to you!

Toasting
1. Bottoms up!
2. Cheers!
3. Drink up!
4. Here's to you!
5. Here's to you and may you have a happy future.
6. Here's to your health.
7. I drink to the future; may it bring us all happiness.
8. I would like you to join me in a toast to the health of President.
9. Jimmy, a toast!
10. On behalf of our president Mr. Johnson, I wish you a happy journey.
11. Let's drink to our everlasting friendship.
12. Shall we propose a toast to the health of our host?
13. To your health!
14. Your very good health, Monica.

 ## Communicative Task

Distinguished Information Desk
Types of Task: pair, class.

Functions Practiced: describing a special event, asking for advice, giving opinions, inquiring, correcting others.

Pre-task

1. You've surely been to many places in and out of your town during weekends, school holidays and public holidays. Recall some interesting, funny, terrible or even horrible experience you have encountered or have been involved in during your trips.

2. Tell your holiday story to your pair and ask for the opinion about the content and story structure. If your pair thinks your story is not funny or not well organized, try either to tell another one or to revise it. Here are some important points you should keep in mind:

1) Use some sequence words like first, next, then and finally in your story telling.

2) Make a sensible choice of words.

3) Make sure the beginning of the story powerful enough to draw audience's attention.

4) Make your ending part unique.

Task Procedure

1. In this task, all of your classmates (except for five referees) will be divided into two or four teams. Each team runs an information desk for tourists at a time and acts the role of tourists at another time.

2. The team that plays the role of inquiring information about the places and attractions is Tourist Team, while the team that plays role of supplying information is Information Desk Team.

3. A Tourist Information Contest between two teams at a time will be held to examine both the accuracy of questions and answers provided and the fluency of English spoken. Here are the rules of contest:

1) Two teams take turns to play the role of customer service personnel at City Information Desk with authentic name labels of the city (town) and the province, and the role of tourists is to ask for any information about the relevant city (town) and the province they are interested in.

2) In each contest, 10 questions should be raised by 10 students, one at a time, in the Tourist Team.

3) The Information Desk Team must also answer those 10 questions by ten different students.

4) Referees, composed by five students from 5 different groups, should be chosen to rate the accuracy of each question raised by the "Tourist Team" and their fluency of English. Ten points will be given to accuracy and another ten points to fluency at each round.

5) Referees should also rate the answers provided by the Information Desk Team for both the accuracy of information (ten points) and the fluency (ten points) in English.

6) Each referee must take turns to declare the scores for both teams at the end of each

round and present a brief comment, if necessary.

　　7) You and your pair must join the same team.

　　4. You and your pair have 6 minutes to work together to fill out the following table **The Places I Want to Visit** with the real information you actually know — exact times and dates of departure, routes, ways of travel (means), the hotel rates (rates), the sights tourists can visit or the resorts they can enjoy and stay for a night. The information must be real and correct. You may need them when you act the roles both in the Information Desk Team and in the Tourist Team.

　　5. In your team, select 10 members to quickly review the information for the accuracy.

　　6. The others work together to decide on first ten questions your team is going to ask during the contest, for example:

> ➤ How much does it cost to fly to Tibet and back?
> ➤ How often does the ferry go to Haikou?
> ➤ Does the morning express to Beijing stop at Tianjin?
> ➤ I am a student in So and So College. Which bus can take me to the Amusement Park?

> ＊＊ These sample questions may not be used in your contest if the contained places are not in your province.

　　7. Now the contest begins. The Tourist Team asks a question and the Information Desk Team has 30 seconds to consult before giving their answer and another 30 seconds to provide the answer.

　　8. Then two teams switch the roles. No short answers are allowed.

　　9. If anything unexpected happens, the referees have the full right to handle it.

　　10. The winning team is awarded the title *Distinguished Information Desk*.

　　11. After the completion of the task, go back to your seats and listen to your teacher's analysis of your performance of the task.

The Places I Want to Visit

Destination	Sights	Date	Time	Route	Means	Fare	Rates